The scorching California sun bakes the dreams of Donald Rawley's characters to such a brittle crisp that they shatter if they're held too tightly. In thirteen dazzling and disquieting tales, Donald Rawley, the acclaimed author of *The Night Bird Cantata* and *Slow Dance on the Fault Line*, exposes these broken dreams and pierces the ravaged lives of individuals who live on the outskirts of acceptable society.

From a Hollywood legend lookalike whose diminutive stature masks a huge craving for love, to a career trophy wife with a gift for pleasing rich old men, to a wealthy Asian matron seeking a precarious salvation through gambling, to two retired hit men reminiscing about the good old days, these portraits offer a searing vision of the dark side of sun-drenched California. As poetic as they are brutal, the stories in *Tina in the Back Seat* resoundingly confirm the late Donald Rawley's reputation as a peerless chronicler of the secret longings of desperate lives.

Other Bard Books
by Donald Rawley

THE NIGHT BIRD CANTATA
SLOW DANCE ON THE FAULT LINE

tina in the back seat

STORIES

DONALD RAWLEY

AN AVON BOOK

This is a work of fiction. Names, characters, places, and incidents either are the product of the author's imagination or are used fictitiously. Any resemblance to actual events, locales, organizations, or persons, living or dead, is entirely coincidental and beyond the intent of either the author or the publisher.

Page 150 is a continuation of this copyright page.

AVON BOOKS, INC.
1350 Avenue of the Americas
New York, New York 10019

Published by arrangement with the estate of Donald Rawley
ISBN: 0-380-80723-8
www.avonbooks.com/bard

Library of Congress Cataloging in Publication Data:
Rawley, Donald, 1957–1998
   Tina in the back seat : stories / Donald Rawley.
     p.   cm.
   "An Avon book."
   I. Title.
PS3568.A846T56 1999   99-27618
813'.54—dc21   CIP

First Bard Printing: October 1999

BARD TRADEMARK REG. U.S. PAT. OFF. AND IN OTHER COUNTRIES, MARCA REGISTRADA, HECHO EN U.S.A.

Printed in the U.S.A.

OPM   10 9 8 7 6 5 4 3 2 1

contents

●

tina in the back seat

the bible of insects

It is commonly known that after mating, the female praying mantis kills the male, eating him slowly, the male seemingly shivering with anticipation, because it is *what happens;* it is the natural thing to do. It is not masochism, this act of sacrifice, but a code, an instinct, a law in the bible of insects that must be followed.

These are the women Inez knows she will never be. They are twenty-four and blond, in billowing beige chiffon, standing in open doorways of their grandfathers' houses. They are used to massive walls of stone, crystal, candlelight, and the smug silence of being better. Inez never had, and never will have, that Grace Kelly chignon, that Elizabeth Taylor white dress, that Joan Fontaine way of craning one's neck so attractively.

No, Inez wears bright colors and big jewels, to make her babies happy, so they don't die in a sea of beige perfection. And she knows she is the one who takes care of these grand-

fathers when those beautiful, billowing girls are too busy
breathing in the night air to take notice.

Inez knows she is the one they whisper about at breakfast,
about how much of the estate that she, a complete stranger,
will claw her way into. Just another vulgar middle-aged
woman, they say, as the hazy Bel Air sunshine hits the
morning table. They do not have to worry. They were born
provided for. And Inez is smart enough to know eyebrows
are raised if she gets too much; lawyers are called.

She is tolerated as a last wish, a foolish dream, like a
tumor that spreads haphazardly, of dying old men. The beige
women say, let her sit with him watching game shows, let
her feed him and tell him dirty jokes and have him write
checks. He is already dead. She is merely taking care of
the corpse.

Let her marry him, change the will, earning her living like
a locust who tears through dry fields. She is more trouble
than she is worth, but she is harmless, and can be easily
bought. Not to worry. She is still a stranger.

These women, Inez knows, will marry men richer than
their grandfathers. They will maintain homes in Palm Beach
and New York and Bel Air and Mexico, and she is just a
cog in the well-oiled wheel, someone who, in time, will disappear, satisfied with the payoff. But she will never be let
inside. She may be up in the old man's bedroom, with
crossed legs and her high heels off, reading *U.S. News &
World Report* out loud as he shakes his head distrustfully.
There may be only one light on, contouring her cherubic
face in a luxurious shadow, and she may put the magazine
down, the both of them smiling warmly. There may be a
moment when she puts on a tape of Benny Goodman, he

loves Benny Goodman, it reminds him of his first wife, and he may turn his head to look out, through the high French doors, into the black night. As he falls to sleep, she may pick up her heels, silently padding across the sculpted Chinese rug to his bed, putting on his nightlight. As she reaches down to kiss his cheek, the scent of her perfume, Orange Blossom, from Miami, Florida, will fill his nostrils, and she will go into the next room, her room, the last wife's room, large and pink and ivory, swathed in silk and damask, and she will prepare for bed, leaving the door between their rooms open just a crack. Soon the sound of crickets in the night-blooming jasmine will permeate these rooms, the sound of a bedside clock whose numbers flip over endlessly, the heavy breathing of the old man and his occasional mumbling of hatcheted memories. But she will sleep soundlessly, without effort, her heavily creamed face shining like a deep lake under the moon.

But she is still not inside. Because the beige women who know this scenario are standing in those doorways of night, their chiffon rippling and their slender hands clutching a drink, but they are looking *out*. Inez is still at the front door, pressing the buzzer, waiting to be let in.

Sarah is one of the beige ones, the only surviving relative, the granddaughter of Inez's fifth husband, Jumpin' Jim Kelley, the corn king of the Midwest, who at eighty-nine is considered the thirtieth richest man in America. Surprising to Inez in an almost evenhanded sort of way, she is also Jim Kelley's fifth wife.

Jim Kelley, like all the men Inez chooses so carefully, has

outlived all his ex-wives, and also outlived his only daughter, Constance, who died an alcoholic.

Constance was dressed in a mink coat and staring straight ahead at a booth at the Beverly Wilshire bar for so many hours someone finally called an ambulance. Only Sarah remains, and she is a very rich young lady with dishwater-blond hair, like Julie Christie in *Darling.* Sarah will live in her grandfather's house until he passes on, which both women seem to be hoping for feverishly.

Sarah tolerates Inez, she knows the score; she has seen three other stepmothers come and go every few years, their purses considerably fuller than when they arrived. She knows old Jim Kelley, whom she has never been particularly fond of, even as a child, has more money than he will ever be able to spend, and if Inez wants a complexion raising three or four million, or even five, so what? Sarah gets two hundred million, and once Pops passes, she's moving to Paris.

Inez does take good care of Jim Kelley, just like she did with Albert and Jeffrey and Bill and Stewart, all of them covered with liver spots and waving at Inez to take her clothes off, walk around the room, jump up and down so her titties bounce. Well, if *that's* all it is, she would say with a sly wink, then I guess you deserve your treat. Afterward, as she leaned over her babies in their sickbeds, the beige ones downstairs quietly moving from room to upholstered room for no reason at all, her husbands would take her chubby hand and kiss it with dry lips, stroke the powdered down of her cheek and say, "Read me some more, open the window, I need my pitcher of water, help me to the toilet."

And Inez, the dutiful wife, helped. No one could ever accuse her of neglect. The most exciting moment, which hasn't yet happened with old Jim Kelley, is that first, deep, dry cough. That's when Inez knows to call, with much fanfare, the doctor for a professional nurse. Then come the IVs and the bedpans. Inez, although wringing her hands in front of the nurse, her eyes liquid with the possibility of tears, would actually walk around her husbands' beds, repeatedly, rubbing her thighs tightly together until she got wet and excited. She could always tell how her husbands knew, their shivering was anticipation, not intense fever.

When the final moment came, Inez was there with the nurse and doctor, and whichever beige one happened to attend, and Inez always kept her face stoic, saddened, but what they couldn't see, these last attendants in these heavily carpeted rooms, was that Inez's mouth was watering, spit sliding down her throat. She was hungry.

Tonight Sarah is downstairs in the living room, French doors open, with a dizzy panorama of Los Angeles and Century City below her. This house is considered the only truly ugly house in Old Bel Air, with too many porticos, balustrades, columns, sculpted miniature trees and yard lights, but what a view.

That's what it's all about, Inez thinks, sipping her nightly bourbon and Coke with Jim. It's all in what you can see below you. That's why she spends more time upstairs, having her needs delivered by the staff; because when she does have to talk to Sarah, she can look down on her as she descends the stairs.

"You want some ice, sweetheart?" Inez asks Jim in a singsong voice. Jim can no longer speak, due to a series of small strokes, his mouth folded into a left-sided grin, spittle running down his chin into a small attached tray. He nods his head and makes a weak gesture with his hand. Jim, Inez thinks, you can't talk but you can sip bourbon and Coke through a straw, can't you, you sly fox. Inez gingerly takes Jim's paper cup and plops two more ice cubes and another two jiggers of bourbon into it, then hands it back, smiling. Jim's eyes light up, and Inez settles herself into her favorite club chair and picks up a copy of *Town & Country*. He'll be out in twenty minutes, she thinks to herself.

Inez can hear night birds cawing in the manicured trees. She believes she can hear black beetles burring under bushes, their wings flapping, a thin musical armor, holding onto Hollywood berries and gardenia bushes already shorn of their blossoms. Sarah probably has those gardenias in one of her priceless crystal bowls, Inez thinks, floating silently until they yellow. Sarah will never hear the black beetles, Inez realizes, but I can. I am able to decipher the love songs of anything ugly that lives in the shadows and bites.

The female praying mantis can be either a dusty green or brown. Known as *mantis religiosa,* because when it rests it lies down on its front legs as if in prayer, it is widely known as a predator who knows how to blend in. This is, again, instinctual. During certain breeding seasons, hundreds of praying mantises can make a fascinating picture, clinging to an old tree, barely distinguishable from its withered bark.

Sarah always seemed to be hovering about now, Inez concludes. She is always at the base of the stairs, seldom going up except to take a bath or go to bed. Inez has it arranged so they do not take their meals together, particularly breakfast, when she might have to answer Sarah's subtle questions in her beige, purring voice.

A coffee is served in the sun room for the two women at about five P.M., and they force each other to attend, smiling archly, trading the hieroglyphics. Sarah goes out for drinks and lunch three times a week with her college girlfriends from Spence and Smith who seem to have landed in Los Angeles, because that's where their family's money *really* is, and besides, who wants to walk through all that slush and dirt in New York or Boston? Of course, no one in their right minds will admit, at lunch, to actually liking Los Angeles, and no one admits to fucking the waiters at all the best trattorias in town, or that they are waiting for their trusts to be finalized and still have to beg their family's lawyers for the occasional advance. Desperation is not attractive.

Today at coffee, the plants in the sun room have been watered and misted, the floor waxed and the silver polished. There are even those little raspberry cakes that Inez will eat five or six of. Underneath the table is a bottle of whiskey to mix in the coffee, and Sarah is wearing an oyster-colored cashmere sweater from Barney's, tan Italian slacks, and sensible flat leather shoes. Sarah is not the string of pearls type; her gold necklace, bracelet, and earrings are from Bulgari. Sarah's hair is pulled up, with a crisscross pigtail braid in back, no makeup except a clear gloss on her lips.

Across from her, Inez sits comfortably in a wicker chair; she is wearing a jungle print housedress and a pull-on turban, mules and her big diamond wedding rings from Jim. She reaches down under the table and breaks open the whiskey, offering some to Sarah first, who accepts, smiling, then pours some into her own coffee as well.

"Nothing like an Irish coffee," Sarah says quietly. The sun casts a burnt yellow fog in the room.

"Actually, we need Kahlua too, but I suppose beggars can't be choosers," Inez says with as much charm as she can muster.

Silence. Both women sip their coffee, easing back into their chairs. Sarah finally breaks the quiet.

"How's Grandfather, Inez?"

"Perky. He gets up and walks around the room a lot. His appetite's good too." Inez's voice flutters in a downward spiral.

She realizes Sarah has been in to see her grandfather only once in the past month. Considering the amount of money Jim is leaving her, Inez feels strongly that Sarah could at least come up for ten minutes every day. Sarah doesn't even bother with excuses; "Oh, it just upsets me too much, seeing Grandfather like this," and other beige songs, never pass her lips. She's a cold one, Inez thinks. She'll die alone. Her children will be wise enough to stay away. Just too busy, Sarah's ancient, shaking hand will someday read on fine stationery; what with Bill's promotion and my charity work, we barely have time to *breathe*. But have a lovely death, Mother. We're thinking of you.

"You've been truly wonderful, Inez."

"He's my husband."

"Of course."

Silence again. A small garden spider crawls from one potted plant to another. Inez watches it with disinterest.

"Inez?" Sarah's voice is probing.

"Yes?"

"I mean, is he *really* all right?"

"You mean, even though he's perky, is he ill? Yes, Sarah, he's ill. He's eighty-nine years old, dear."

"Of course." Sarah's reply seems downtrodden, curious, even eager. "What kind of illness is Grandfather experiencing, Inez? It isn't painful, is it?"

No, Sarah, Inez thinks, no pain. No morphine needed. No possibility of the new will being rejected under the possibility of duress or of not being in sound mind and body. Inez has already been through that little drama with Stewart's stepdaughter from a previous marriage. What was her name? Eileen. How could she forget? An out-of-court settlement from Inez, and Eileen went back to Montana or wherever she came from. Inez remembers how Eileen approached her outside the lawyer's office, tears in her eyes, saying she did it for her three children, so they could have a future, to which Inez coolly replied, "*I* did it for love."

"Not painful at all, Sarah, just a creaking of the bones, I suppose. But Jim has great spirit, you know." Inez can see the trace of a scowl on Sarah's face, and is amused.

Don't you realize, Sarah, that your grandfather loves me? Inez muses silently. We have experienced a satisfying passion that only age and time create. I am forty-nine years old, with large brown eyes that Jim Kelley said reminded him of mink, and you know, silly girl, he bought me two minks to match my eyes. Had the furrier bring them right up to the bedroom, so I could select. Jim doesn't care that I'm heavy and my breasts are too large. He likes them big, likes for me to take them out and rub them on his face, likes to close his eyes and feel my nipples on his eyelids, then passing over his mouth. And I love him. I love his body, ancient and spent. I can see how broad his shoulders must have been,

and I put an arthritis cream on them every night, very gently
so it sinks in the right way. I massage his old feet and legs
and tickle his privates and feed him his medicine and I make
sure he eats only the food he loves, like fried chicken and
chili and coleslaw and chocolate pudding. He gets his bourbon every night, he does whatever his heart desires. Because
I love him. We have *an understanding,* something the beige
ones will never have.

Sarah taps her nails on the table, pours herself some more
coffee and reaches under the table for the whiskey.

"Don't drink too much coffee, Sarah, you'll never get to
sleep."

"I'm going out tonight."

"Oh, I see."

"On a date. Grandfather's business partner; have you met
Teddy Goddard?"

"Yes. You're going out with Teddy Goddard?" Inez asks,
disbelieving. "Teddy Goddard is eighty-seven years old."

"God no. His grandson, Turk. Turk's a stockbroker."

"How nice."

"No, Inez, I'm not following in your footsteps." The air
becomes stale.

"That was an unnecessary remark, Sarah. As you go on
in life, you'll discover there are many reasons to marry.
Companionship. Love. Intellectual stimulation."

"Money."

"Yes, money makes a difference, Sarah."

"You must be a very wealthy woman by now, Inez."

"Yes, I am."

Sarah purses her lips. Inez stares very hard at her and it
frightens her.

"Am I not allowed to be wealthy, Sarah?"

"No, I didn't mean it that way."

"You know, dear, wealth is a privilege, not an expectation. Some people actually work for their money."

Sarah purses her lips again. Inez thinks, Oh, you've got *that* down pat. You'll be pursing your lips like that for the rest of your life. God, how many men you will make miserable with that tight little smirk.

"You should marry many times, Inez."

"Too many already." Inez waves a fly away from her forehead and begins to smile. "I have noticed your grandfather seems to be very congested. We should call in his doctor the next few days."

Good news. Inez studies Sarah. She can see Sarah thinking. How long the legalities will take, what kind of taxes she will have to pay, who she knows in Paris, who she will have to write to, asking for certain introductions.

Sarah's head snaps up as Inez's voice gruffly whispers, "See, little girl, I don't do it for the money."

"Then what for?"

"Because I enjoy it."

Now a throbbing silence. Sarah sets her coffee cup down noisily on its saucer. The sunlight is dimming.

"I see."

Inez's tone completely changes.

"Well, tonight Jim and I are going to play Monopoly. He always wins, you know. Of course, I let him! But then, I have to remind myself I'm playing Monopoly with a man who made a fortune dealing in corn! What do I know? You know, Sarah, all my husbands, all the men in my life, were self-made men. They never relied on anyone but themselves, never waited around for the prize. They had already stolen it! They have always seemed to understand me, and I them."

Inez looks at her ten carat diamond wedding ring and smiles. The afternoon sun has hit it just the right way, spinning light patterns and shadows on the interior wall of the sun room. All Inez has to do is tilt her finger slightly and a new kaleidoscope seems to emerge. It is a game, Inez thinks.

Sarah watches Inez play with the reflection of her diamond. Inez doesn't care; she has a box full of big diamond rings from big-time men who spawn spoiled mistakes like Sarah and Eileen and others, and no, she doesn't care.

Sarah gives Inez a curious glance, and gets up from the wrought-iron table. The spider Inez saw earlier has moved on to a third pot and disappeared into a thick tunnel of leaves.

"You and Grandfather have a good time tonight, Inez. I don't think there's anyone quite so kind as you are."

Inez blushes as if she believes her. She feels she may have said too much to Sarah, but isn't concerned. Sarah is like all the beige ones, the well-bred girls before her and after her, their mothers and aunts and cousins and school friends who cling to a tree, never flying, fed easily and expecting their due without ever thinking they wouldn't get it. Because they always get what they want.

Inez rises and slowly trudges up the stairs. She feels she is getting too fat, her thighs thick and little veins appearing around her feet. A little extra weight and you never have wrinkles in your face, Inez notes. In the right light, the light of old men's bedrooms, you can look like a dream for years.

It is three o'clock in the morning and Inez is awakened by the sound of crickets and something else she cannot put her finger on. Getting out of her bed, she goes to the old man's door and listens. It is a full moon outside, firing up her bedroom in a blue light. She opens the door further, and stands in the doorway, listening.

Then she hears what she's been waiting for. The dry, hollow cough, the thinning blood, the lumps that are beginning to form. She sees Jim in his bed with his nightlight on. She goes to the bathroom, wets a washcloth, then gingerly sits on the bed next to him, gently patting his forehead and cheeks.

His eyes are sunken, terrified. He coughs again, blood coming up in his spittle. Inez kisses him on the lips very slowly, then runs her tongue along the outer rim of his mouth. Jim suddenly smiles, and Inez is pleased. She then walks over to the phone and dials emergency 911 for an ambulance. Time being of the essence, she walks down the hall in her pink nightgown and knocks on Sarah's door. A surprised voice answers.

"Who is it?"

"Sarah, it's Inez. Please get up." There is enough seriousness in her voice, she knows Sarah will be at the door, and quickly.

The door opens just a crack.

"Yes."

"Jim's starting to die." Nothing more needs to be said.

Sarah's eyes glaze over. She is not quite sure of what to do, Inez can tell.

"I've called for an ambulance. There's not a great deal of time. Please get dressed and then come to your grandfather's room."

"Turk's here," Sarah says in a whisper.

Inez can do nothing but sigh. "Get rid of him!"

"All right. Of course, you're right, Inez."

"Meet me in fifteen minutes. And turn the house and yard lights on. And notify the staff."

Back in Jim's room, Inez closes the double doors and locks them, smiling at her husband. She watches his convulsions, his shivering and his mouth opening to speak her name silently, and she thinks, Oh Jim, now is the time, the house will be full of light and sirens and this is all we have, the last great moment, when all hunger is appeased; watch me, darling. I will lead you by the hand as the crickets chirp and my beetles burr, into the garden, to the trees and the sky, and Inez leans back against the double doors, watching her husband's eyes roll up and back again as he tries to focus on her, and she shimmies and arches her neck, slowly lifting the folds of her nightgown above her hips, like curtains parting for the first act of a show.

baby liz

Baby Liz has just stepped down from her RV, and it is a long step, particularly as she is only three feet tall, an exact yard and no more, her mother used to say.

She has just driven into Los Angeles from Tucson, where Baby Liz performed at the Desert Gem and Mineral Show. First she did a scene from *Cat on a Hot Tin Roof,* with her specially tailored white slip, then threw on the full makeup and did *Cleopatra.* The rest of the week she modeled big cut topazes and aquamarines, always pretending they were diamonds. The dealers loved her. Baby Liz could sell anything.

People pointed. Children giggled, middle-aged men leered, but Baby Liz didn't care. She was getting paid, and was an exact replica of Elizabeth Taylor, in miniature. Like anything porcelain that costs money. Baby Liz even had that flutter in her throat for those dramatic moments.

Baby wants nothing more than to breathe in the air of her new home, a town house in the San Fernando Valley. She notices there are many rosebushes in the complex, and they seem to be bursting, as though they were confused by the warm February weather. It's nice here, Baby Liz reasons. Full of flowers, auto exhaust, the occasional child on a bike, taking solitary flight. It's everything she imagined Southern California would be.

Baby Liz has realized over the years that it is all a matter of commodity, and she has something no one else has. She's a one of a kind, and as far as she's concerned, that's the best kind to be.

She often thinks of her grandmother, from Russia, who was only two and a half feet. Her grandfather wasn't much taller, an elegant man with a silver-tipped cane and a book of Russian poetry he wrote before the Revolution. She still has the book. It is charred from a bonfire. Her mother was average height and they never got along. Baby Liz doesn't mind.

Now, at the age of forty-one, after three failed marriages and a string of cross-country affairs, Baby Liz is tired. She has enjoyed the open road, but she feels it is time to settle down, and has bought a small but nicely decorated condo in Canoga Park.

She has put up a For Sale sign in the RV's window and has already almost sold it.

The almost buyer was an elderly man and his wife, who stopped, amazed, when they saw Baby Liz.

"What?" The old man seemed confused.

"Why it's *uncanny*, it really is," his wife said, beaming. It was no big deal to Baby Liz. She took them aboard and also showed them her book of eight-by-ten photos.

"Well! Look at this, Harry. She looks just like Liz Taylor in *The V.I.P.'s!*"

"One of my favorites," Baby Liz whispered sweetly.

"Oh! And here she is in *Ash Wednesday,* Harry."

"Ash who?"

"Dear, it was a film about a facelift. We all went to see it in the seventies."

"One of my favorites," Baby Liz quietly said. "It wasn't marketed properly, you know."

The elderly woman, hand on her replaced hip, looked around the RV.

"You've done this up real cute."

"Thanks."

"Say, how do you drive this thing?" Harry looked at the driver's side controls and chair, which swiveled.

"I have attached rods that I push down with my feet, for gas and brakes. They'll come right out."

"Uh-uh." Harry didn't sound convinced.

"I've gone cross-country in this RV seven times," Baby Liz said proudly. "Never one accident."

"Does the car have a name?" the elderly woman asked.

"Yeah, I call her the *Butterfield 8,*" Baby Liz cooed, fluttering her heavily mascaraed lashes and attempting her very best White Diamonds smile.

"I like it, Harry. It's well-maintained."

"I'm not so sure. We'll let you know. We got a couple more to see, but we have this new phone number in Canoga Park."

"That's right," Baby Liz said. "I'm retiring."

"Good for you. See, the way I know it's a new phone number is we live in Van Nuys and for years the first three

digits for Canoga Park were always the same, but now
they've come up with some new ones. . . ."

Baby Liz smiled.

"How interesting," she said in a tiny, round voice. The
old man realized there was nothing more to be said, saluted
Baby Liz, and smiled, showing long sharp teeth.

"I like it," the elderly woman whispered to Baby Liz as
they left.

The elderly couple never bought the *Butterfield 8.* A pair
of young gay men bought it for full price and Baby Liz was
thrilled. On one condition; in her photo book they asked to
keep a photograph of Baby Liz as the call girl in *Butterfield
8.* She wore a slip, a mink coat (which she found in the little
girl's department at Bergdorf Goodman many years ago on
her only trip to Manhattan), and that bitchy little sixties flip.
Oh yes, and pointy spike heels.

The two men couldn't stop giggling. They gave Baby Liz
a red crayon and asked her to sign it. She of course obliged,
writing "No Sale" across the photograph, and the two gay
men were ecstatic.

"Oh my God, we'll put it over the driver's seat. It's a
shrine. A temple!" the younger gay man, with a bald head,
said as he pinned it up.

The young man left and Baby Liz turned to his older
friend.

"He looks very handsome with a shaved head," she said
sweetly.

The older friend turned and looked at her.

"He's on chemotherapy. This is our big trip. We're just
going to keep on going, you know?"

Sunlight streamed through the Irish lace curtains Baby Liz

had put up in the RV. She turned and looked sweetly at this man, maybe thirty-eight, with the beginning of a paunch. A nice guy, a million of them on the road. She took her tiny hand and stroked his.

"You coming back?" Baby Liz asked. There was a long pause. Dust pulsed in the air.

"No."

Baby Liz reached up and kissed the man on the cheek.

"Well, you remember this. Wherever you both are going, the *Butterfield 8* will get you there. And in grand style too."

Baby Liz openly wept as her RV was driven away, the two men waving and blowing her kisses.

"That's one hell of a piece of machinery," Baby Liz said out loud, as though offering a psalm to the late afternoon. Palm blossoms drifted around her. "She was one of a kind."

Baby Liz is enjoying her early retirement. Every few weeks her ex-husband Sidney, number two of three, calls her up and they talk. She knows by the tone of his voice he's itching to move in with her again.

"You stay in Seattle, Sidney," Baby Liz laughs, "and don't come knocking on *this* door anymore."

"Ah, honey, c'mon." Sidney is the only husband of hers that is a little person as well. The rest of them were huge. All Norwegians. Husband number one was named Rolf. Husband number three was named Tangen. And the affairs . . . well, she admits to herself now that she must have been some sort of a Viking queen in a past life. Norwegians. Go figure.

It's the quiet that she likes now. She can always tell Sidney's voice. He's the only one that calls.

"Hiya Baby."

"Hiya Sidney."

"You still the most beautiful woman in the world?"

"Always, Sidney, always."

Baby Liz likes the sound of her mantel clock, very fancy and French. It's a tiny, high ting where the hours make their mark; elegant, the sound of a beautiful jewel falling on marble. Or the last moment in a symphony when a chime, or a triangle, is struck, saying that's it, the most delicate is always saved for the last.

She loves her new dining room set, a Duncan Phyfe six-seater that she bought at auction, along with a crystal chandelier. Once it was delivered and installed, Baby Liz spent two full days soaking it with lemon oil and changing the fabric on the seats to a beige silk damask. Baby Liz wants lots of candlelight and flowers. And good lighting. And lots of champagne.

Sitting one night watching *Wheel of Fortune* and eating a Weight Watcher's Fettuccine Alfredo, Baby Liz realizes she doesn't know anyone here in Canoga Park, so after dinner she goes over to her next door neighbors, whom she knows are a young married couple with a five-year-old son, and knocks politely on the door.

A little boy answers it. He's a sweet little brown-haired muffin, with long lashes and sunburned skin. He stands looking at Baby Liz, transfixed. All his child's energy is suddenly subdued. He cocks his head. Baby Liz cocks her head and smiles. They are exactly the same size.

"Hi," she says brightly.

"Hi."

"I'm your next door neighbor. I wanted to know if you

and your mom and dad would like to come over tomorrow night for dinner.''

The little boy is terrified.

"Mah!'' He runs out of sight. "Mah!''

Within moments his parents are at the door, maybe twenty-five, twenty-six tops. Nice kids. His father is a sandy-haired muscular guy, a real hayseed, in a dirty jogging suit. His mother has the same brunette hair as the boy, pulled up in a messy chignon. They both stare at Baby Liz, their mouths open. They do not blink.

"I'm your next door neighbor. My name is Elizabeth. I'd like to invite the three of you over for dinner tomorrow night. How about it? I don't know anyone here.''

"That dining room set. You just got it. I saw it delivered. Very nice.'' The mother smiles openly, suddenly relaxed, and jabs her husband in the side with her elbow. This invisible signal, Baby Liz notices, gets him to speak.

"Sure. Great,'' he says, extending his hand, which she takes demurely. "My name is Neil. This is my wife Susan, and this is our son Jamie. Short for James.''

"I don't like James,'' the little boy says, grabbing Baby Liz's hand away from his father.

"Wow. That's a really big ring,'' the little boy says, awestruck.

"It sure is, honey,'' Baby Liz says confidentially, then looks up at his parents. She knows they don't have much. "We'll have roast beef and champagne. So how about it? Eight o'clock.''

The young woman is laughing.

"We'd love to. Absolutely! Can I bring anything?'' She seems almost giddy.

"Bring James's favorite soda pop."

"Grape! Grape!" James interrupts.

"Bring him grape."

Baby starts back to her front door, then stops, turning around, and crosses her arms, studying Neil.

"And incidentally, the boys have to wear a coat and tie. When men have dinner with me, men wear a coat and tie."

"Yes ma'am," Neil says.

It is six months since Baby Liz had Neil and Susan and Jamie over for dinner, and Jamie and Baby Liz have become great friends, taking walks around Canoga Park, going to Disney movies, having pizza at the Sherman Oaks Galleria.

Jamie holds her hand wherever they go, and she always compliments him on being such a gentleman. She knows how people stare, and it seems Jamie likes the attention. Made for show business, this little boy. She even goes so far as to suggest to Neil and Susan that Jamie would be good for commercials, to which they agreed eagerly, but they still have no clue as to how to start.

Today Jamie and Baby Liz are walking through a vacant lot behind a closed Ralph's market.

Baby Liz loves all the shortcuts that she takes with Jamie. It's the child's road, full of dirt lots with wildflowers and frightened cats. Sometimes they find things, like a small suitcase still packed with a girl's clothes, and socks, and hair berets. Jamie and Baby Liz make up adventures for the suitcase. Where it's been, where it might be going. Baby Liz can't explain to Jamie that it could imply something evil. Evil is not allowed on their walks.

"Will you be my girlfriend?" Jamie kicks a pebble as they

walk, and Baby Liz feels uncomfortable in all her makeup. Too sunny, too dusty. When she gets home she knows she'll have to take her face off and start over again.

"You're too young."

"How old do I have to be?"

"About thirty years older, honey."

Jamie pauses, and looks at her.

"I'm serious."

"So am I."

"We could go to the circus. Run away."

Baby Liz begins to laugh.

"Well, sweetheart, I've married a couple of clowns, that's for sure. But my act is a little too sophisticated for the circus."

"What is sophisticated?"

"When your mom and dad get dressed up and go to a party? That's sophisticated."

"Oh."

A dust devil is coming in the hot valley wind.

"Look, there's a twister," Jamie says to Baby Liz. "And it's not any bigger than you! Go on, Elizabeth! Jump in it!"

"You've got to be kidding."

Baby Liz watches the tiny twister move toward her. She stands perfectly still, daring it to mess her up. It doesn't. Bits of newspaper and styrofoam cups fly past her. The twister skirts her, moves on and dies out on Vanowen Avenue.

"You should have jumped in it."

"No, I shouldn't have."

"I love you, Elizabeth."

"No you don't."

Baby Liz tenderly strokes Jamie's right cheek.

"You know, you're already two inches taller than me. In the next ten years, Jamie, you'll grow to full size. You'll be double my size. You won't be so interested then."

"Yes I will."

"No you won't."

Baby Liz pauses, withdraws her hand and takes a Marlboro cigarette out of her handbag and lights it.

"Can I have a puff" Jamie asks.

"No."

"Who is Elizabeth Taylor? Mah says you make your living as an impersonator. Mah says an impersonator pretends to be someone else. Why do you want to be someone else?"

"Jamie, I am who I am."

"Who's that?"

Baby Liz thinks for almost a minute, in silence. She runs her hands through her hair and drops her Marlboro in the dirt, covering it with her high heel.

"I am a beautiful woman."

Jamie nods his head. From the perimeter of the vacant lot Jamie suddenly sees a Doberman running toward them, without a leash. The dog is frothing at the mouth. Jamie screams. The Doberman stops about six feet away from them, growling, baring its teeth. Baby Liz turns and looks at the dog.

"Get in back of me, Jamie," she says in a whisper.

Baby Liz focuses on the dog, who is ready to lunge. Her voice becomes raw, loud.

"Who's afraid of Virginia Woolf? Virginia Woolf? Virginia Woolf?"

The dog, still snarling, perks up his ears. Baby Liz spits out at the dog.

"You're a goddamn nobody. Maybe Georgie boy doesn't have the stuff! Maybe he doesn't have it in him! A great big fat flop!"

The Doberman stares at Baby Liz. He stops snarling. He is confused, lowering his neck.

Baby Liz's hair falls in messy strands across her face, and her lips curl downward in disgust. She cackles.

"Look at you. What a nobody. A big goddamn nobody."

The Doberman, courage back, snaps futilely at Baby Liz.

"Don't touch me. Don't you dare touch me, George. Just what the hell do you think you're doing? Liar! Liar! Cut it out, George!" Her voice has risen to shattered glass.

The Doberman begins to cry quietly, and paws the dirt, then runs away from Jamie and Baby Liz.

"Good," Baby Liz sighs.

"How did you do that?" Jamie asks.

"Oh, sweetheart, it's some lines from an old movie, not for kids. Works like a charm every time. See, Jamie, when you're small, you have to stand up to people who are bigger than you. Because they're cruel, and most times they're stupid too, like that dog. Because you'll be smart, Jamie, and you'll be a kind man. I'll see to that. And when you're real, real old you'll remember me."

Jamie takes Baby Liz's hand.

"I'm going to buy you the biggest diamond in the whole world."

"No you won't." Baby Liz smiles. The wind is bringing up too much dust, and she coughs.

"So where you want to go now?" Jamie asks.

"Let's go have an ice cream where I can sit and comb my hair."

"Okay."

Jamie and Baby Liz look up to the sky. Its blue is clear as a Caribbean shallow beach, seen from a plane, and Baby Liz takes her other hand and points up.

"Never stare at the sun, Jamie. But around it, if you look hard enough, you'll see stars. They turn white at night. But during the day, they're angels with blue wings. They're everyone small, and helpless, and they keep a lookout for you. And me."

"I want a raspberry-pineapple cone," Jamie says quickly.

Baby Liz realizes he doesn't understand what she's saying, and she shrugs.

"Remember, Jamie, angels with blue wings."

"I'll remember," Jamie says with disinterest.

Baby Liz's ring, a very large cubic zircon that is an exact replica of the Krupp diamond, or so she's been told, sparkles in the sun the way Richard Burton would have wanted it. Her fingernails are pink and polished.

They will pass wild mustard weed, and mint in thick patches, and Baby Liz will make a mental note to cut some for a salad.

"And I want chocolate fudge," she whispers as the two shuffle through the next vacant lot, to a place where there are trees, and neighbors, rosebushes that bloom confused, dining room tables soaked in lemon oil, and childhoods that never end. A place where Baby Liz has settled and grown like a vine, with violet, sweet flowers, honeybees and tangerine trees, pictures of her glamorous career in silver frames, and her second ex-husband, Sidney, still calling, romance in his distant voice.

the tiger's tooth

"Wong, you in?" The voice is male, Chinese, high-pitched yet gruff.

In very elegant Chinese, Gloria answers him, "Yes. It's Mrs. Wong, Herman. You know how many Wongs are in this world? About twenty million. First name, Gloria. I played here for two years, Herman, and I know your full name."

Herman slowly inhales his cigarette and blows smoke through his nose toward the great jeweled ceiling. He nods to the waitress.

"Wong's in. Get her a drink."

Tonight the lighting is just right; a pearly glare on the table and just enough glimmer in the background to keep the action interesting. Gloria Wong knows this to be a good omen. She knows she will lose what she can't see, but when the light is good, nothing can stop her.

Gloria first came to the Tiger's Tooth Club for poker and bingo. Safe stuff. Poker she liked but it was too slow. And bingo! Too many old women winning toasters and cheap Japanese televisions like the one in her kitchen. No thanks.

Then she discovered Pai-Go. Gloria loves the sound of chips, made of cow bone or sometimes good ivory. Their sound on the table lingers like a pulse, a fever of memory that makes the small hairs on her arm rise, alert. Pai-Go is blood every night, Gloria thinks. High stakes under a ceiling encrusted with twisting gold dragons from Hong Kong. Gloria loves the plastic palms, the nicotined wallpaper, the incense, and the constant, low luxuriant hum of vice.

She has watched businessmen from Macao and Singapore lose ten million dollars with one swipe of the chips. She's watched them tremble and become stiff as a corpse, having to be lifted in their chairs by several men and put outside until the cold sea air brings them to their senses.

This was in Hong Kong, on a floating restaurant and casino. They had faced one man to the sunrise. He was a statue. After the first rays of dawn, he stood up and jumped off the boat into the China Sea. They were several miles from shore. Gloria has often wondered if he was able to swim ashore. If he could, she knew he would put on a fresh change of clothes, shave, and come back to the boat the next night.

California doesn't understand Pai-Go, and the Chinese keep it to themselves, and play for big money behind closed doors. Now, in Las Vegas, Gloria loves the big, public, anything-goes Pai-Go rooms in the Chinese-only casinos; talk about glamour! But like an alcoholic to rotgut wine, Gloria always comes back to the Tiger's Tooth, for their brand of Pai-Go, in this Los Angeles suburb called Gardena, which reminds Gloria of every other suburb she's ever been in with the name "Garden" to start with. Garden Hills. Gardenhurst. Garden Mile. Only no gardens. Ever. Just industrial buildings and tired two-bedroom tract houses. Maybe a rosebush comes up every hundred years or so, just for spite. Gloria dreams, her eyes glazing over slightly. She imagines how if she pricked her finger on one of those sad thorns, her blood would turn to wine.

Gloria adjusts her red Chanel jacket and waves her hand toward the girl's shoulder. Her Chinese becomes clipped.

"I want a double scotch. But it's got to be Dewar's, because Dewar's goes gold in the glass. Lots of ice, a dash of salt. Lots of ice, tall glass. If it's not gold, I'll send it back."

"Huh?" The waitress seemed confused. She is a nice Asian-American girl, probably a freshman at college. The girl offers a young smile. Gloria turns to Herman, then to the waitress. Gloria taps her nails on a table in staccato. She speaks in English.

"Don't you understand full Chinese, young lady? Shame on your parents. Herman, this girl shouldn't be at a Pai-Go game. It's not right."

Herman stubs his cigarette and lights another. Smoke comes through his teeth as he smiles. Like a demon's breath; Gloria gazes, stunned, one eyebrow arched.

"Give her a double Dewar's in a tall glass, Bernadette, lotta ice." The waitress understands and begins the traces of a smile.

"Sure. Double D. Got it." The waitress, relieved, scurries out.

"Bernadette?" Gloria asks with a stoic face and leans over the table.

"She's my half sister's third daughter. You know how the Catholics are."

Gloria leans back in her chair and studies Herman Wu. She has never liked this wrinkled man, who chain-smokes. He reminds her of her husband, Jack Wong. Thirty years come October, Gloria has been married to Jack Wong. They have two daughters, Lila and Natasha, both in college.

Over the past two years at this casino, Gloria has learned Herman Wu's name too well. He has hounded her credit card companies, her bank managers, people who should respect Gloria but now do not.

Herman always gets his money. Gloria smirks at the thought of Herman Wu ever actually losing money. He'd be frantic; an utterly confused coward. It's the balls he lacks, Gloria muses. Jack was strictly for breeding. He's out to pasture now, still unclipped and enjoying his life, but Herman? She almost feels sorry for Herman Wu. Gloria knows she could make love to him, out of either pity or desperation, but she wouldn't eat for a day for fear of throwing up. Then Gloria remembers that the Tiger's Tooth, over the past two years, has milked her assets to the tune of $300,000. Sure, she does win, but most of the time, like everyone else, she loses.

This is what she hates. Losing like everyone else. Blending in. Just another Chinese matron from Glendale, California, who gambles too much. She suddenly imagines Herman Wu naked, in the throes of ecstasy, and giggles.

"What's so funny?" Herman Wu stubs his cigarette out.

"A memory. Nothing more."

"You got a lot of memories, Gloria."

"And a lot of money, most of which I've lost here."

"Comme ci, comme ça."

"Why Herman, how . . ."

"Elegant?"

"I wasn't thinking of that word exactly, Herman, but it will do."

"Tally up."

Gloria looks around the table as Herman barks out his orders. An eighty-year-old Chinese woman, whom Gloria guesses comes from Shanghai if just from her jawbones alone, takes out a small alligator suitcase full of hundred dollar bills. She pushes it across the table and speaks to Herman in a lilting mainland accent.

"Hundred thousand dollars. Pai-Go will treat me good."

"Sure, honey."

A sweating young Chinese man in an Italian sweater and thin, round, tortoiseshell glasses takes out a suitcase. It is slightly battered. He pushes it across the table.

Herman clicks the case open, pauses, studies the young man. He speaks in Chinese.

"This money looks dirty to me, kid. Looks like it needs to be put in a washing machine."

"Hundred thousand dollars, like you said."

"I don't think so. Then we gotta hang it up to dry, in clean air. There's no clean air in California. Maybe in Texas, though. All this costs money, kid."

"Hundred thousand. Like you said."

"Eighty thousand."

Herman does not blink. The young man wipes his forehead.

"Okay. Eighty thousand."

Gloria has seen this young man before and wonders how much money he has embezzled. Half a million? He looks so sweet, like an architecture student who will build his wife and children a spare, large, and terribly modern house somewhere in Orange County. Or maybe La Jolla! Gloria knows these should be the dreams in his head. Watching him is an entirely different experience.

She will never fall that low, no sir, because she knows when to stop. She knows when to stop when she loses, and she knows when to quit happily when she wins.

Herman, with the fine grace of a rattler, turns his attention to Gloria.

"You got a hundred thousand, Mrs. Gloria Wong?"

The waitress sets down her drink. Gloria takes a long sip. Its steam cools her cheeks.

"I'll write you a check."

"We don't take your checks anymore, Wong."

"I've got some credit cards."

"You maxed those out last week, remember?"

Gloria's heart is beginning to shake. That can't be. She paid them off on Tuesday.

"Yeah, I remember."

She takes off her wedding ring, a nine carat marquis diamond in platinum. She tosses it across the table.

"Nine carats at *least* a hundred thousand."

"At least a hundred thousand to whom?" Herman snaps.

Herman takes out a jeweler's glass and studies the ring.

"Fifty thousand."

"Okay." Gloria nods her head. Herman drops it into a tin box.

Clink. One of the ice cubes in her scotch cracks in half just as the ring hits tin. Good sign, Gloria thinks.

"What else you got?"

"I got a 'ninety-six Rolls outside, black with beige leather, loaded, perfect condition." She tosses the keys to Herman.

"Forty-six thousand," he says.

"You're crazy. That car cost over two hundred thousand."

"Cars depreciate."

"Mine don't."

"Oh really, Wong? Does that mean anything you park your ass in goes up in value?"

Gloria pauses and sips her drink, her eyes steel.

"Why yes, Herman, it does."

"Forty-six thousand."

Gloria sighs.

"Okay."

"You wanna play at ninety-six thousand, or you want to work one hundred?"

"A hundred thousand, of course."

"Then you owe me four thousand."

Gloria tosses a watch at Herman. He sniffs.

"Cartier. Common as clay in Hong Kong. One thousand."

Gloria's eyes begin to fill with tears.

"I don't know if . . ."

"Three thousand left. You got a change of clothes in your two-hundred-thousand-dollar Rolls-Royce, Mrs. Wong?"

Gloria is trying to hold back her sobs. She half shakes her head.

"Yes. A T-shirt and jeans. And sandals, I think."

"You know, my wife has always wanted a red Chanel suit like that. I know she's just your size. Those shoes alligator?"

Gloria nods her head.

"That ritzy-bitsy handbag alligator too?"

Gloria nods her head, looking down at the floor. Suddenly this light is too much for her. Herman signals his assistant, a gaunt, shadowy man never far from the table.

"Ed, go get Mrs. Wong's playwear. You go change, little lady, and you're on for a hundred thousand."

Gloria rises and kicks off her pumps, handing them to Herman, who grins. She dumps the contents of her alligator bag on the table. An uncapped lipstick, a strange plum red she is not sure she likes, calling it "unsure" red, rolls across the table and onto the floor, leaving several marks that look like blood. Blood and Pai-Go, Gloria thinks as she breathes in deep. That's why I come back every night that I can.

"Wait." Herman's voice again. Gloria turns around and faces him.

"Matching wallet with handbag. Fair is fair. We put the rest in a paper bag. We don't want you to not have your identification."

"You remind me of my husband, Herman." Gloria walks toward the women's rest room.

Herman laughs. "See you, Wong!"

The teeth and claws of a tiger, when ground into a fine powder, are believed to restore a man's sexual vigor. Illegal throughout the world, Asians for centuries have hunted for the tiger tooth. Now this powder is very expensive, and generally fake. The powers it promises are always a gamble.

That's why this cruddy little casino is called the Tiger's Tooth, Gloria thinks. She feels a bit smug, knows it is a defense gesture. The casino is full of impotent old men losing family fortunes.

Gloria also knows that in one bite, if done at the appropriate angle, a tiger can completely sever a human head, just like a guillotine. Gambling is a hunt, Gloria reasons. We want the powder of the big cat, we never get what we want.

Looking at herself in the ladies' room rococo style mirror, framed in white jade camellias (although Gloria is positive those camellias are just cheap soapstone from Korea), she is a beautiful woman. Gloria puts on her jeans and T-shirt and she can see the heat come on. Her eyes are on fire.

Gloria knows Herman Wu's wife, Miriam, and thinks, well, at least I don't take secondhand goods. I may lose them in a gamble, but spoils are for lesser women. My husband still has tons of dough. I have a copy of the nine carat marquis in cubic zirconia. Jack will never notice. He hasn't looked at my hands in years. Never even notices a new nail polish.

Gloria looks at her long, perfectly manicured nails, the hallmark of a rich woman, and sees she has painted them sangre d'beouf, like the dripping glaze on good Tang dynasty pots. Oxblood. Blood of the bull. Gloria laughs.

She points to herself in the mirror and shakes her finger accusingly.

"You are a very, very bad girl. You lose tonight, you lose it all."

Gloria gets closer to the mirror to freshen her eyes. She touches one of the camellias on the mirror's frame. Her palm lingers over the petals of the blossom, how the jade is strung together to create a full, bushy camellia. She strokes the bloom quietly, listening to the rattle of jade petals, and real-

izes it sounds like the click-click of Pai-Go. And these flowers *are* white jade, old, from the mainland, probably Peking.
Another good omen. The discovery of white jade by touch.
She touches the flower one more time, lets down her hair,
which is luxuriant, black and straight. She thinks, I look
fifteen years younger.

She can hear the old woman's stiff Shanghai accent in
the hall.

"Come on, Wong. We haven't got all night."

"Oh yes we do," Gloria says quietly to the mirror. She
applies her "unsure" lipstick.

"I'll be out in two minutes!" Gloria yells through the rest
room door, then blots her lips with a tissue.

Gloria suddenly remembers saying this thirty-one years
ago, when she was dating Jack. She was going to a technical
college in San Francisco and only had enough money for a
one-room apartment, with a refrigerator and a hot plate. But
it had a beautiful blue and green tiled bathroom from the
thirties, big and opulent, that obviously must have belonged
to the much grander apartment next door, which was a three-
bedroom. She spent a lot of time in that bathroom.

She remembers how Jack would tap his watch. Knock on
her bathroom door.

"Hon, we got the dance at the club. It's dinner and I think
it's already started. C'mon Gloria."

She always made sure when she emerged, in a sky-blue
silk or cream peach linen dress, that she was perfect. Moist
lips, shining hair. A touch of Chanel No. 5 on the shoulder
and behind the ear. Jade or pearls. Very conservative. That's
how she got Jack Wong. Gloria realized a long time ago,
right after their honeymoon in Rio (Jack had wanted to go

to Honolulu to pack in a couple rounds of golf. How common), that she would have to maintain this level of perfection. She thought, Well, if I have to be one of those kind of women, I'll do it all the way.

All her girlfriends from high school had moved down to Los Angeles, and they were surprised to find out each had exactly the same life. One evening, in the library of Gloria's Tudor home in Glendale, the girls began to keep score.

How many husbands played golf? All of them. How many husbands in medicine, real estate, shopping centers? All of them. How many reminded the girls of Asian Jimmy Stewarts? All of them. How many with white blond mistresses tucked away across town or in another city? Gloria remembers a hush descended over the room, then sudden shrieks of hysterical, girlish laughter. Hands were raised. All of them.

Miriam Wu was there, Linda Li, and a wonderful, funny woman, Anette Wing, who died in a car crash a few years later, when her Cadillac convertible went off a cliff in Palos Verdes Estates. Gloria still secretly believes it wasn't an accident. And Connie Lo, Elizabeth Yu.

Gloria still lunches with Linda Li on a regular, twice a month, basis. Always the same food, French, at a little bistro in Encino. The only time she ever eats Chinese is at Jack's family's house. That way she can ooh and aah over the dishes and seem almost sincere.

The girls gambled, played numbers, bridge, then started having some real fun: currency speculation. Gloria liked currency speculation, but it was a lot of work and she preferred a game with a set of rules. Rules that can never be broken. Because otherwise there's no game. Ten years ago she asked

Jack and Bob Li about Pai-Go, and they shook their heads
and fingers in front of her, stern expressions on their faces.

"Bad news, Gloria," Bob Li said, finishing the rest of his
Manhattan. "Game ruins lives. Like opium. Bad all the
way."

Gloria noticed Bob Li was getting hefty even then, drinking all those sweet, gooey Manhattans. Now Bob is huge.
Has to walk with a cane. Poor Linda hasn't been sexually
active in years.

But Gloria has. When she found out about Jack's mistresses, four to be exact, over the last seventeen years, she
went out and found herself a good-looking Armenian lawyer,
a really hairy guy, and they lasted for a good ten years.
Affairs can be cruel, Gloria thinks now. But they can also
be a hell of a lot of fun, and they always end. That's the
plus. How they end is another story.

The old woman bangs the door with her cane.

"Move it, Wong!"

Gloria emerges, smiling, and looks down at the old
woman, who is dressed in a sequined and bugle beaded
jacket, in shades of gray and yellow. Very 1982, Gloria
thinks.

"So how much are you going to lose tonight, old dear?"
Gloria whispers in the elderly lady's ear. They quietly walk
toward the Pai-Go room, the high stakes room, the room of
death and good lighting.

"I'm going to win all your money, you prissy little Los
Angeles bitch, and I'll send it back to the mainland." The
old woman says this at perfect pitch, so only Gloria can
hear. She laughs.

And Gloria laughs with her. The two women sit down at

the Pai-Go table, their concentration solely focused on the chips, the table. Immense double doors of mahogany inlaid in ivory, very highly polished, are closed with barely a trace of sound, or air.

In two hours the sweating young man is out. He goes into the parking lot and tries carbon monoxide poisoning through an air vent in his BMW, but a security guard, knowing this old trick, smashes his driver's window and pulls him out. The security guard roughs him up a bit, tells him he's going to call the police, and then sends the young man speeding away in his BMW. A note is delivered to Herman Wu, who reads it, tosses it into a wastebasket across the room, never taking his eyes off the game.

"He'll be back tomorrow," Herman Wu says quietly. The air from the chips makes his cigarette smoke flutter.

Gloria is unconcerned. She has been winning all night, big money. Suddenly she stops. The fever is beginning to ebb. She knows she has to stop.

"Give me my money, Herman, I'm done. It's after midnight and I have appointments in the morning."

The old woman does not look up at Gloria. She will lose it all, Gloria knows, and probably stay until dawn.

"Three hundred thousand, Wong."

"Goody, goody. How much to buy back my wedding ring, Herman?" Gloria leans back in her chair and crosses her legs.

"One hundred thousand."

"Okay."

"And the Rolls?"

"One hundred fifty thousand."

"See, I told you, Herman. My personals go up in value."
Herman smirks. "What about the Cartier watch?"

"Oh, you keep it for Miriam."

She watches Herman Wu's face very carefully. He slightly
flinches, and it gives Gloria a happy glow. She'll unload too
many good women's things on Herman. Miriam will be back
on her prescriptions in no time. She knows he will never say
thank you. He's not in the thank-you business.

Swiftly his composure returns. A natural reflex for this
little reptile, Gloria decides.

"And the suit and shoes and handbag?" Herman's voice
sounds suddenly meek.

"Maybe next time we play strip Pai-Go. I only wear Victo-
ria's Secret, and those items are terrifically overpriced."

Gloria rises.

"Well, you take all that home to Miriam. Put it in a pretty
box. And be careful, with such pretty gifts she might suspect
you of being with another woman?" Gloria's smile dazzles.

"I have plenty more of those silly suits at home," Gloria
says in very elegant Chinese, waving the common odors of
Herman Wu and the Tiger's Tooth as far away from her as
possible. "So fifty thousand, the car keys, the ring, Herman!
I really must be on my way."

Herman tosses the ring and keys to Gloria, counts out fifty
thousand dollars.

"I always say, Wong, fair is fair."

"Of course you do, Herman."

Walking to her car in the brisk Los Angeles night, Gloria
can hear the sounds of light traffic on the freeway, which
now after midnight is almost an echo. Gloria likes the early
morning hours. They are simple to her. You have either won

in the last day or you have lost. At two o'clock in the morning in Los Angeles, there is nothing more to be said.

As she turns to put her key to her car door she lightly cuts her fingers. Quickly she puts her finger to her mouth, and is not surprised to find that tonight her blood tastes sweet.

Driving home to Glendale, the lights of the giant freeway lamps pass over her emotionless face like river water over rocks.

Gloria begins a list. Jack will be home tomorrow afternoon from his business trip to Tucson. She knows dinner will ensue. Tomorrow morning she will have her hair done, stop by Rodeo and march into Chanel and buy two new suits, maybe a bright yellow two-piece and then something very schoolgirl, in navy and white with lots of tiny pockets and brass buttons. She does get so terribly tired of red.

Her mouth slowly forms a smile. She'll go to Elizabeth Arden and have her face done too. And perhaps some pretty gold earrings with black pearls. Gloria presses a button and rolls down both front windows. The wind on the freeway is misty and cold. She lets her hair fly around her in the dark car, and makes a note to invite Miriam Wu for lunch. She wonders what Miriam will wear.

the closest thing to god

Some of us search for God in the woods, and some of us find God under the living room sofa. Some of us, the pilgrims among us, search in dense cities and small towns, but in the long run we either die young or we die old, and that's when the desperation begins. If only He will give us a sign.

Iris is forty-seven years old, with black hair and a full face, and she is searching for God, and making no small talk. There is a place where He will make himself known. What Iris is unclear about is where, and whether all will be forgiven when the meeting takes place. Iris tried to become a nun, but the crew cut and tattoo of Elvis scared the Sisters away.

Iris has always been butch. She drives an ambulance with another woman, a heavyset number named Genevieve, pronounced in full. They eat at Tommy's Burgers on Beverly Boulevard on Mondays and Wednesdays; Tuesdays and Thursdays it's Little Joe's down in Chinatown.

Iris is always gruff and cheerful and the paramedics love

her, particularly when blood is squirting, the sirens are rolling, and in a booming voice Iris suddenly starts singing, "I love the night life, I like to boogie." It cracks them up. Saves a lot of lives. No tension.

She has searched, in her own private world, the faces of the dying and the almost dead, and sees nothing but vacant pain. For the first year her dreams were horrifying, as Genevieve said they would be, with lack of breath and the nasal rattle of death. Then she relaxed, turned in for a good black sleep. That was five years ago. She's fine now.

Iris tried Genevieve on for size but it didn't work out, and they're just buddies, going out for beers in Silverlake. Actually, the closest thing to God Iris has seen has been a chick named Dot, who hangs out, beautifully, at the Two Ladies Club. Dot has long legs and high heels and measures a full head taller than Iris.

Iris doesn't know what to say in front of Dot. The hazy blue smoke of the bar makes Dot look like a Raymond Chandler heroine, and Iris knows no matter what the lighting, no matter how much smoke, she's still going to look squat, crew cut, with the beginning of jowls. A girl like Dot, well, she wouldn't even consider her.

Until one night when Iris decides to give Dot a gift. A small gold pin, real gold, of a question mark.

"I just wanted to let you know I've kept my eye on you. I don't know how to really meet someone like you," Iris says with lowered eyes, "so I thought I'd buy you a little something."

"Someone like me?" Dot whispers in a feathery voice. "I'll tell you right now, what is your name?"

"Iris. Iris Jones."

"Well, Iris, I got a girl. She's over there playing pool. Her name's Cheryl."

Iris turns around briefly and sees Cheryl put a striped ball in a corner pocket. Muscular arms, short hair, a cigarette in her mouth. Tough customer. Then, not really giving it any more thought, Iris turns back to Dot.

"So, are you going to accept my gift or not?"

"Well, I'm not sure—"

"Oh, go on." Then, as if to add spice to the proposition, "It's real gold."

Dot stares blankly at Iris. Iris suddenly notices Dot's eyes, made up and as green as jade, and large. Big cow eyes. Iris knows she could lose herself in those eyes, throw away the key. And Dot's lips, thin but well-formed. In fact, perfect. Little pearl earrings. Pink lipstick and a touch of blush.

Dot shifts on her bar stool, crosses her long legs and lights a fresh cigarette.

"Now why would you be buying me gold when you don't even know me?" Dot asks strangely, a little shocked.

"Because." Iris shrugs.

"Ah. I see. Well, I'll accept your gift, Miss Iris Jones, but I'm not opening it here. Not in front of Cheryl. She keeps an eye out on me."

"I bet she does."

"But I thank you for your thoughtfulness and I guess now we're not strangers."

"Yeah."

Iris walks away, shrugging and smiling. Her face has gone red, and she downs a bottle of beer, then decides to get good and drunk, and orders a double scotch, then another, and a third. The air around her smells like women she will never get, angels in smoke with muscular arms and good teeth. She just bought a gold pin for a woman she doesn't know, and it doesn't bother her a bit. Warmed by scotch and the sway of the darkness, Iris begins to sing, first under her breath, then louder, and even louder.

At home, a tiny apartment with a galley kitchen and hardwood floors, Iris flops on a sofa she found in the street and moved up to the third floor all by herself. In fact, most of her furniture is from the street; broken tables she repaired and refinished to a high gloss, a color TV in an old sixties console that she had fixed for cable. But she's always in the ambulance, or at the Two Ladies, where she's still waiting to see Dot walk in, get a nod and a half smile from her in the blue, shimmering shadows, and Iris keeps thinking, Somehow. Sometime. It is part of finding God; falling in love, Iris thinks. I'm just as worthy as anyone else.

Iris's mother, Lorna, was a bombshell. When Iris was growing up in the fifties, Lorna wore tight dresses, tightly curled platinum-blond hair, and a heart around her neck a sailor had won for her on Santa Monica pier. Father had cleared out for all points north, San Francisco, where he was later arrested on vice charges.

But Lorna was never woe is me, Iris notes with satisfaction. Lorna taught Iris how to be tough. She said it was the only gift she could really give Iris, because it was the only thing she was good at. Lorna was wrapped so tight in her blue satin and her black velvet, almost showing stretched seams, that Iris often thought when Lorna was with a man and took her clothes off, her voice must change.

Lorna knew Iris was a lesbian from childhood on; as she

pointed out, Iris wouldn't have to rely on some fucked-up man to eat anything; a cheap Italian dinner, a hot dog, oh God knows how Lorna hated cheap men. Iris also wouldn't have some squalling brat at her tit, Lorna mumbled proudly, the ashes from her cigarettes scattered on the floor.

Iris remembers her mother in a gray shuttered light. The blinds, wherever they lived—and they lived in quite a few places as Iris grew up—were closed permanently.

"Sunlight. Forget it. I'm a night person, Iris. My skin is white and I'm keeping it that way." Lorna stirred a Manhattan in the kitchen. She liked stem glasses, drinks with cherries and olives, a little glamour. A reason to be; to sit at her bar and sip, do her lips, meet a man or two.

"You're out in the sun like a man, Iris. Well, I suppose it can't hurt you. But you're eating too much, Iris. There's nothing worse than a fat tomboy."

"I'm not fat," Iris said, knocking her knees against the kitchen table.

"If you're fat, forget having girlfriends, sister." Lorna narrowed her eyes and gave Iris a kiss, then stood up, pushing out the wrinkles in her tight blue satin dress, the one with a sweetheart neckline, and downed her Manhattan.

Iris began to blush. Her mother knew, and Iris wasn't sure if she was relieved or not. Lorna went to a mirror by the kitchen telephone.

"Hand your mother a beer out of the icebox, and get one for yourself too."

Iris was only fifteen.

Lorna winked at her. "It's good for you. You might as well learn."

At the kitchen table, under a white light that made Lorna look like a well-made-up corpse, Iris listened.

"I believe in God, Iris. And so should you. You should go to church. Oh, it's my fault, I guess, but you can feel real good when you talk to God, Iris. If you're lucky you'll meet him, and God's a guy, Iris, a good-looking guy, not some old poop with a beard on a cloud."

Lorna tapped her nails on the table and said softly, "Or, in your case, I guess a girl will do. But you gotta be *aware,* Iris. Sometimes it just goes. You don't know you met God, and boom, it's all over, not even begun. So you got to keep your eye out, little sister. You know, Iris, you're no beauty, but if you do what's in your heart, well, it's the only way to go. You're worthwhile, baby. And you'll find God."

Lorna was to leave Iris for good when she was sixteen, moving on to better things with a car salesman from Topeka, named Francis S. Small. Iris cringed, stayed tough, got along on her own. Lorna sent letters in a spidery scrawl, generally the scrawl becoming more difficult to decipher as her drinks piled up, and Iris threw the letters away. Now, over thirty years later, sitting in her tiny apartment, Iris is glad. She doesn't believe in clutter and boxes full of paper. Who needs it?

Iris is in the desert, at a little motel with a kidney-shaped pool that a lot of the girls at the Two Ladies recommended. Halfway down a two-lane between Palm Springs and Indio, Pepper's Motor Lodge, even though a simple motel with a pool, has tried everything to be a *resort.* Stan and Fran Pepper have built a tennis court, put in exotic clusters of palms and cactus, and a big shady bar, on the honor system, by the pool.

Stan and Fran are deeply tanned, the lines in their sagging skin lined horribly from the sun, and Iris realizes that now Stan and Fran *have* to stay out in the sun. God knows what they would look like otherwise. Stan and Fran's uniforms are tennis outfits with green lining, and Iris seems to notice they always have a drink in their hands, never a tennis racket.

Iris likes the desert, the clarity of its heat, the way its smoky purples creep in slowly at dusk. How you can stay outside all night long and breathe easy. Some of the girls are sitting out by the pool this afternoon, and Iris is sitting in a pair of shorts and a cutoff T-shirt. She has put on Bain de Soleil and thinks, Today I'm going to bake my chops, get the smell of the ambulance out of me, get that look of disdain off of Dot's flawless face. Iris still can't get Dot out of her thoughts. It's been six weeks since she gave Dot that gold pin. She's seen her at the bar, crossing and uncrossing her long, gorgeous legs, and not even a nod to her. Iris sighs, turns up her transistor radio, and falls asleep under rustling, dry palms.

In her dreams she is a man, always a man, muscular and sharp, a gentle man, climbing mountains and building small boats. It is a recurring dream, a cockatoo sitting on his shoulder, all the money he needs, and a dog at his feet. But no woman. He lives far away from any women.

When Iris wakes there is an iridescent green lizard on her shoulder, studying her. She flicks the lizard away—and turns her radio off, then looks at her skin; good and pink, it'll go brown in the morning. It's almost the start of twilight, and at the outside bar, thatched roof with bamboo walls, a group of girls have congregated for margaritas. One of them waves

Iris over. Iris nods her head, and goes wearily to her room to change.

When she emerges, Fran Pepper is tinkling the ice in a rum and Coke and winking at her.

"Is something wrong?" Iris asks.

"Not at all, honey," Fran says, her eyes twinkling. "Stan just thought you might want to see our tourist attraction. You can tell everybody back in L.A. I'm telling you right now, you won't see anything like it, just behind your room, actually. Just follow me, honey."

Fran leads Iris through the dusky air, a light wind blowing Fran's hair, to an enclosure, a chain-link cage, long as a dog run and about twelve feet wide.

"Get a load of this," Fran whispers. In the cage are the largest, most horrifying lizards Iris has ever seen, some of them up to eight feet long, snapping at flies and bobbing their heads. Iris watches their tails move through the sand.

"The big ones are monitor lizards, from the north of Mexico. Closest things to dinosaurs I've ever seen, honey. And the red and blacks with the butt heads are Gila monsters. Long tongues. Boy, do they bite."

A Gila monster tries to climb the chain-link fence near Iris and falls, turning over several times until it rights itself, then looks up at Iris and begins to hiss.

"Most of them are girls, if lizards can be girls and boys. Eggs hidden everywhere, lots of catfights over eggs," Fran says in a confidential tone. "Just like women, right?"

Iris turns and stares at Fran Pepper. Fran pays no attention to her. "Soon we'll open a lizard ranch, Jeeps and all, like Lion Country Safari, next to Pepper's Motor Lodge. We're talking big money." The ice in Fran's drink clinks like a wind chime.

Iris smiles at first, then begins to cry. She tries to hide her face from Fran, who adjusts her prescription sunglasses.

"I'm sorry, honey, sometimes you girls get upset. Well, you know the way back. I'll leave you be."

Iris touches the chain-link fence as though it is electrified. She watches a Gila monster flick its long tongue and catch a big desert horsefly. The lizard closes its eyes for a moment, its tail moving like a dog's, then opens its eyes again, staring directly at her.

Iris lightly rattles the chain-link fence, thinking, It's all a matter of fences, cocks, things imprisoned and breeding unsuccessfully, waiting to be released. Perhaps to God, or no one at all.

Ashamed, she wipes the tears from her eyes and notices the lizards are staring at her in the mauve shadows, hissing, flicking their heavy tails. Iris begins to laugh.

"All right, then. Which one of you ugly bitches will let me buy her a drink?"

It is three months later and Iris has bought a Harley-Davidson motorcycle with a gas tank in high gloss purple and black, framed by a line of yellow-orange flames. She loves her bike, considers the bike a girl, like certain cars, and has nicknamed her "Rosie," after Rosie O'Donnell.

Tonight, on a black Los Angeles August night, Iris has parked Rosie in the front of the Two Ladies, right where the streetlight hits the wall near the front door. Rosie shines and glistens just like a new motorcycle should. Iris thinks, She's the best looking thing in town, and she's all mine.

Dot is sitting at the bar, and her girlfriend, Cheryl, is

deeply involved in a pool tournament between four women, an event the Two Ladies sponsors every second Thursday.

Iris slides up to Dot and orders a whiskey with a beer chaser, and Dot doesn't even acknowledge her. Dot never starts the conversation, Iris thinks, and I'm not starting one. But she could at least nod her head at me, a little smile couldn't hurt, after all.

Iris moves away, drinks in hand, to "her" table, where she can keep her eyes on Dot, even though she won't admit to it, and also see the rest of the action in the club.

Lately a beaner chick named Gloria has been hanging around Iris, and tonight Gloria collapses into a chair at Iris's table. Iris likes her, not enough to bed her, but she likes her curly black hair, the shaky earrings Gloria always wears, her rose red lips and overly made-up eyes. Iris laughs at Gloria's jokes, buys her as many drinks as she can handle. In return, Gloria makes sure Iris is never bored.

"So how's Rosie, Iris? Keeping your cunt warm?" asks Gloria, sipping on a margarita and batting her false eyelashes.

"Rosie's great, Gloria. Riding smooth. Beautiful sound to the engine."

"Well, I'm pooped. I stayed up till four o'clock with a bunch of broads at one of their houses. Never drank so much in my life," Gloria sighs, "and I shouldn't be here. I should be asleep."

"Your call, Gloria. You're here."

"That's right, sweetheart. Waiting for the same thing you are." Both women laugh. Gloria continues, her eyes glazing over. "You know, I pray to the Virgin Mary every night, light candles to Saint Theresa and Saint Bernadette, and I say, 'Girls, how come I can't get laid, fall in love with a good woman?' a woman like you, Iris."

"You think I'm a good woman?" Iris asks, her voice soft.

"Yeah, sure, baby. But you're not interested in me. You don't even know what you're looking for, but you're looking, that's for sure."

Iris laughs. "I'm looking for God, or the closest thing, in a dump where well drinks cost a dollar. I keep thinking a shaft of light is going to come down, Dot will appear before me and kiss me on the lips, and everything will be explained."

Suddenly Iris turns her attention away from Gloria and concentrates on Dot. A young butch chick, with rings in her nose, a crew cut, and a tattoo of a dragon going up her arm and onto her neck, has sat down next to Dot and begins to make shy conversation. Dot stares ahead, smokes her cigarette, sips her drink.

She's like me, Iris thinks, only younger. With better chances. Iris watches the little dyke become more confused and agitated, suddenly bringing out a small wrapped box and setting it down in front of Dot. Iris peers through the smoke and reads the young girl's lips, then Dot's.

"I want you to have this. It's real gold."

"Now why would you do that? You hardly even know me."

"Yes, but we could be friends, right?"

"I gotta tell you. I have a girlfriend named Cheryl. She's over there, playing pool."

Iris can see the little dyke looking down at the floor, her face red, tears forming in her eyes. Then a couple of women move in front of them, blocking Iris's vision. Iris quietly exhales. She feels suddenly calm, and looks over at Gloria, who is hunched over her margarita with cold teeth and a grimace.

"Want to go for a ride?"

Gloria shakes her head.

"No way, Iris, you drive too fast."

Iris rises and pats Gloria on the shoulder, then walks out to Rosie, who's waiting there under the streetlight, her new chrome twinkling like ancient rays of sun.

Rosie's riding like a dream, and Iris can feel her growl, contented. In back of her, somewhere in Van Nuys or Panorama City, she can hear the drone of an ambulance with full siren, echoing through the dusty avenues. I'll start working tomorrow, Iris thinks, I'll go back to the bell of death, the driving through stopped cars, the oxygen pumping, the jokes from the front seat.

Someday I'll be in the back of one of those ambulances, gliding under the palms like a cat with its tail pulled, and that's when God will appear. Another woman will be there to hold my hand, and I will be old, insensate, mumbling.

Iris likes the fast August night hitting her face and rubbing the top of her head. It's all a series of offerings, gifts, Iris thinks, prayers for buyers and sellers. Well, not you and me, Rosie. We'll find God yet, girl, His hand is on my shoulder and in your wheels, and He's sitting out there like a panther, waiting in the dark.

mother of pearl

Los Angeles is bursting with bad men named Hector, Armando, and Paco, with eyes like a glass of Kahlua and sharp teeth. They have tattoos of mermaids, and crossed knives above the word MIEDO, and their arms are muscular and scarred.

They are men at fifteen, corrupt at eighteen, sometimes dead at twenty. They have moist lips and a way of walking that clears sidewalks. They are perfumed with Jockey Club and Aramis, and they hold the scent of limping women on their fists.

And they'll hustle you out of everything you've got. Because Los Angeles is a town built by hustlers, for hustlers, and left in wills to hustlers, bad men with loins so stiff they have to dance and fight to keep them down. When they finish with you, whatever room you might be left in reeks of them, whatever room you're crawling out of with wobbly legs from too much sex and a dry throat that won't disappear.

They like fast cars, late nights, guns and knives. Girls named Suzy who swallow, with fishnet stockings and a real American accent. Sometimes they'll want a man who's got money, who's debauched enough to do as they say. And sometimes they want a kiss that lingers.

I cannot give any of these things. I am forty-five, a pretty young man who faded in middle age. Now I am poor, shy and lonely, living in a small apartment with a view of an alley. The doctor tells me there is a shadow on my lung. How I've wanted a strong man to wrap his arms around my skinny shoulders until I can't breathe. How I've wanted his come to shimmer on my chest, every slow thrust an innuendo and a trance. How I've wanted him to promise me his soul.

But I have nothing to trade. Watching the bad men strut like parrots with their wings clipped, I know nothing comes for free. Something is taken. As I see their heads crooked for sex, I say never for me. No, not ever for me.

I am taken to a welterweight fight in East Los Angeles, past an overgrown park and a graveyard where hibiscus is growing out of graves. It is in an ancient two-story warehouse. Felice Garcia versus Angel Jesus del Toro. Past Cuban cigar smoke and grime, past men with gardenia oil in their hair and dirty white polyester suits, I see Felice Garcia on his stool, his mouthguard in place. He's staring right at me. His eyes are a sable brown, and I cannot catch my breath. He is too beautiful, too young, too pure for me.

His arms are very muscular and there is a small tuft of black hair on his chest. He smiles at me, in the second row, scratches his nipple and wipes the sweat on his purple satin shorts. He shifts his legs, as he thinks I might be able to see up his shorts. I cannot, but I pretend I can.

My friend Henry hands me a paper cup with bourbon in it. I hand it back.

"I don't drink," I say quietly, not taking my eyes off Felice.

"What *do* you do?" Henry asks with a leer. "You into Mexican food? You into big hot burritos?"

I turn and look at Henry. He is seventy-five and obese, with pink skin and a penchant for ex-cons. One shot at him and missed, another stole all his furniture. Someday, I know, he will be murdered. He's dancing toward it with glee, and he frightens me.

I am ashamed to be here. I am too effeminate for this crowd and I have to guard my gestures, make sure I don't cross my legs the wrong way. Straight men generally sit at games with their legs spread and shoulders slightly hunched, as if they're sitting on the toilet. This is the posture I assume.

Angel, with a pug's face, a crew cut, and bullet-hole eyes, walks proudly into the ring, holding up his arms. The crowd applauds. Over an echoing loudspeaker an announcer, speaking in a velvety, rapid Spanish, introduces the fighters, and the bell rings.

"If you want to see real blood," Henry says to me, "in two hours there's a cockfight. Two mean fucking roosters. You've never seen anything like it."

"Why do you think I want to see that?" I ask, annoyed. Henry shrugs.

"Because you like danger," he shouts over the roar of the audience.

"No, I don't," I say to myself, watching Angel Jesus del

Toro hit Felice so hard blood trickles out of his mouth and slides over his nipples, some of it getting caught in his chest hair.

Felice must be about nineteen, I reason. I like how his thick hair shakes as he does the boxer's hop. And how his muscles are tense and lean.

The crowd begins screaming invectives at Felice in English, then in Spanish. Two middle-aged women behind me are in a rage over Felice. They sound like bluejays fighting, cawing in a Castilian lisp.

"No. I'm sorry, but I don't like this at all," I say as loudly as possible to Henry, who glares at me and turns his attention back to the fight. I know this is the end of our friendship, which was a minor one at best. I get up to leave, but at this moment Angel punches Felice with such ferocity the oil from his hair flies on my face. I am suddenly flushed, my eyes bright.

It is the most singularly exciting sensation I have felt in ten years. I run my hands along my face, and watch Felice, who, as he crumples to the floor, smiles at me and closes his eyes.

"You took quite a punch," I murmur soothingly as Felice comes to on a rickety cot. It is close to midnight. I have waited in this dim room for four hours. Felice had been thrown in here after the fight, then just a few minutes ago an ancient Mexican with no teeth and an Elvis Presley toupee threw water on Felice and broke an amyl nitrite ampule under his nose.

The boxing hall is empty, as is the old warehouse. Elvis

Presley nods to me as if to say, "I'm leaving now, *maricon*. You take care of the bastard. You lock up."

Felice has been stripped out of his purple boxer shorts. He is wearing a red jockstrap. I'm amused. I wonder if he keeps leopard skin bikini briefs at home.

"You. Come out of the shadows. I can't see you." His voice is deeper than I imagined.

I am not sure if I should walk into the light of the bare bulb in this makeshift locker room. He will see that my hair is falling out, that I am thin, white-skinned. A stutterer, a whisperer. Ready to be picked over. Like a corpse in the desert.

I walk into the light. Felice's pubic hair is flaying out of his jockstrap. He wiggles his feet and smiles.

"What lonely eyes you got, baby." He wipes some dried blood away from his ear with a curious expression, then wipes it on his cot.

"Where did you learn English?" I ask.

"El Paso, Texas. I saw your lonely eyes. You're bad for Felice."

"I should go. I was worried," I say quietly.

"But they're pretty eyes, baby." Felice tries to yawn, but it hurts. "Oh shit, that dog fucker hurt me. Son of a bitch has no dick, thinks he's a big man like me."

Felice looks at me with a satisfied smile.

"You want Felice, don't you, baby? Felice is expensive." He gets up stiffly, in a sore heave.

He stands in front of me. He is exactly my height, but he seems so much taller.

"What time is it?" he asks, touching my cheekbone. His hand is thick, almost rubbery. I look at my watch.

"Ten minutes to midnight."

"Jesus, you stay here all that time for me? You must *really* want Felice."

I realize now I have gone too far. I should sink back into the shadows, find the door leading out with the back of my hand. I should find my friends, others with shadows on their lungs and broken hearts. I should try driving at night, to no place at all, with my doors locked and my windows rolled up.

"What's your name?" Felice asks, running a finger along my chin.

"My name is Claude."

"You French?" Felice asks, cocking his head.

"No."

Felice shakes his grogginess off and gestures toward a filthy sink.

"Take that towel, wet it. You rub the blood off me. Okay? You're my new friend, right?"

"Right," I say.

As I rub his shoulders and chest, the lightbulb flickers above us.

"You take me out for tequila tonight, okay? And hamburgers. Loser don't pay, loser never pays. I saw you got a watch. I lost my watch."

"It's a cheap watch," I murmur. Felice grabs my arm and looks at it, then takes it off my arm and puts it on his.

"It tells time. You got some money for Felice?" His voice is reptilian.

I stop rubbing his chest and look into his eyes. His eyebrows are spiky and black. One eye is beginning to swell up.

"No, Felice, you probably have more money than me."

"You old whore! *Viejo puto!*" He coughs, spits some saliva and blood into a tin can. "Okay, I pay for tequila and hamburgers, but you do as I say. Later, you make Felice come. Okay?"

I nod my head slowly. I don't know what to say, and I start rubbing his chest again. I imagine Angel is with his manager and his plump girlfriend with teased red hair. Angel Jesus del Toro won't remember Felice Garcia tomorrow morning.

"Where are you from?" I ask. My questions sound high-pitched, like a nervous woman. One loser confiding in another.

Felice doesn't mind the question. He smiles at me, then closes his eyes and licks his upper lip.

"I was born in a corral in Tecate and walked to Acapulco when I was ten. Open those doors." I walk over to a set of heavy, industrial cast-iron double doors and open them. They swing out to a second floor fire escape.

Below us several Cadillacs and El Caminos are parked near a liquor store called El Bambino. I can hear salsa playing from not one boom box, but two or three. Same song and channel. I can see a crescent moon, peach-colored in the dank Los Angeles night, and a sky punctured by stars.

"What are you looking at? Get back here, lonely eyes."

I turn and walk back to Felice, who looks at me coolly. I begin rubbing him. He wants to talk.

"There was old men and young boys like me, little baby horses. I was the most popular. I stay at the El Presidente, at Las Brisas with the guys. There were coins to dive for.

There were old gringos with white shoes and flowers on their shirts, big wallets. There was a boat, I know, ready to take me away."

"To Hollywood?" I ask archly.

"Yeah, baby, Hollywood. But first El Paso, Dallas, then Ensenada. Yeah, Felice *es muy popular.* Going to be a movie star." He laughs.

I suddenly imagine Felice in a tourist villa at the top of Las Brisas, twelve or thirteen years old, hair just beginning to grow under his arms, holding a candy cane from Christmas. He's sucking it carefully in the Mexican sun until it's a sharpened spike, then puts it in his jeans for later.

I see him dive naked into a tiny round pool as baby cockatiels test their wings and banana leaves quiver. "You gonna finish me?" Felice asks, grabbing the towel away from me. "You dreaming, huh, lonely eyes?"

I step away from Felice and stare at him in silence. I am too frightened to say anything foolish.

Felice is built like an attack dog. When he moves he crunches his shoulders like a wrestler, little man with big balls. I bet he comes all day and dances all night, snapping his fingers at waiters and pimps. And I cannot stay away.

Looking at Felice and seeing bruises suddenly appearing on his hips and shoulders and arms, I want to kiss him. I realize I am the imprint on a shroud, my face's oil and sewn lips only leave a hard metal mark for Felice to decipher.

Felice balances himself as he stands up and stretches, then pulls his jockstrap down, kicking it off with one foot. Lazily he knocks the lightbulb and it swings on its cord.

"You like Felice? You like big Felice?"

I nod my head. He walks over to his cotton pants and takes a penknife out of his pocket. I lower my head. So this is the trade. A watch for a knife. A blow job for a stab wound. I become frightened.

"Don't back away. Touch it. Touch my knife."

Felice ambles up to me. I can feel his penis against my leg. His knife has a mother of pearl handle and it is warm in his hand, in front of my face, doubled up like a fetus, its handle glowing dully. I can smell Felice, and it is overpowering, like sewage and rose water and heavy fog.

A mambo is drifting up from the street. Felice clicks the blade out and rubs the handle slowly on his chest to make it shine, then tests with his thumb the serrated edge of the blade. Then lightly rolls it on my neck, my chest. He cuts two buttons off my shirt, and whispers in my ear.

"I cleaned abalone in Ensenada with this knife, faster than anybody. You gut it, one cut and it flips on this big wood table. Then it doubles up, no noise. Just like a heart. Just like loving me, lonely eyes. No noise. Like a fish out of water that dies, when rainbow comes up on its scales. I washed a thousand shells in river water, sugar, and sun. The pearl rises, shining like your eyes, old man."

I realize there are tears in my eyes. If this is my last embrace then I will fall into it. Felice raises and cuts off a lock of his hair. He throws his knife at a cork bulletin board, empty of bulletins, where it sticks. I feel like I'm going to pass out. Felice takes my waist with a swollen hand; with his other hand he throws his hair on my face and shoulders like confetti, laughing.

"Now you belong to Felice. You never leave."

*   *   *

The mambo from the street has gotten louder, more rapid. It's Tito Puente and Celia Cruz. It's playing from open windows in crowded apartments where the smell of molé sauce drifts past the palm trees and stars that dot my peripheries like talismans. Felice's cock is pressing against me like a mariachi's golden guitar, pulsing like a high tide. Like a winded sunset in the desert. Like a heart.

"You like to dance? Felice will teach you how to dance, *el baile,* baby." I see how welts are rising on his head and neck. Such black curly hair he's grown to make him a man. A vein leads from his loins to his hard belly. Next to it there is a lil' devil tattoo with a baby's ass and a tail, pitchfork, and smirk.

Felice undresses me and it dawns on me that I am naked too, old, unkept. I cannot decipher what will happen, but I tenderly put my hands around Felice. I am careful not to touch his bruises, but he still winces in pain.

"You wrinkled old man," Felice says, breathing heavily. We are pressed together, moving our hips slowly, and I know Felice does not see my sad little chest, my scrawny legs. I put my hands further down, around his buttocks, and look up into his eyes.

It is midnight and I am not poor and sick and old anymore. I am moaning. Felice is listening, his teeth clicking like a rattlesnake and his hair still on my skin.

"See, lonely eyes, when you dance, *en el baile,* you got to hold the girl close. Like this."

saigon

Life's a desperate thing. That's what Virgil told me and I didn't believe him. He said once you put your money on the table you never get it back, and living through a war was like roulette. Virgil explained that being maimed was like casino credit, and if he looked hard enough, he could always find somebody pretty for good luck. To stand next to him while he won.

I knew Virgil for two years. I hear him now, when the sun becomes too bright and people stay inside. Or when I am alone in movie theaters.

That's where I first met him. It was a Wednesday and I was sitting in an art movie house in Encino. In the sapphire half-light of the theater, a blond woman with an expensive haircut and beige slacks wheeled in a red-haired man with no legs. There were small American flags attached to the rubber handles of his wheelchair. They were laughing together. I could smell bourbon around them. I was a recovering alcoholic, and the smell of liquor made me alert. I never realized how it could carry.

I spent a great deal of time alone, in air-conditioned movie houses in the middle of the San Fernando Valley. Every day of the week. I chose restaurants at off hours so I could sit alone. I was frightened. Mostly of myself.

I didn't want to drive my car into another wall, or wake up on a beach fifty miles south of Los Angeles after a blackout drunk. I didn't want to have to remember how to not be effeminate, how to fit in every day.

It seemed the correct thing to do. As a lonely child I promised myself I would never be on the outside looking in when I grew up.

The couple's laughter became muffled giggles upon seeing me. As though they realized they had to be quiet, like children at a matinee of old ladies and strange men.

They sat directly in front of me, which I found annoying because the theater was empty. It was a bargain matinee of *Indochine* with Catherine Deneuve. I loved Catherine Deneuve. I wanted to see her being remote and perfect, absorbing the light the way real movie stars do, and giving nothing away.

The red-haired man grinned at me. Then he clutched the back of the seat in front of me, from his wheelchair, and hoisted himself up, grabbing the back of the seat in front of him, so he hung suspended, the rest of his torso swinging in dark air.

"How's it hanging?" he said to me and laughed. It was difficult to enjoy his joke. I nodded my head and smiled.

On his wedding finger was a horseshoe ring with grimy diamonds. His eyes were a stained blue, a bachelor blue, as though the sky had leaked its color unto him as a gift, or a warning.

His blond friend couldn't figure out how to close up his
chair. She peered at a clasp and tried to yank it. She tsked
several times, her agitation steely and muted, her hands frantic. Several strands of hair brushed across her nose and she
swatted them away. The red-haired man arched his neck to
one side and bellowed.

"For Christ's sake, Ann. There's a button on the side."

His arms were exceedingly muscular and I realized he
probably lifted weights. I knew he had a lot of spare time.
As his blond friend found the button and walked up the aisle
with his folded wheels, the man continued to swing. He
watched me and pretended to do exercises.

"You should see me on a diving board." He studied me
to see if I would laugh. I didn't. I was uncomfortable being
around him, because he was maimed, and it was just one
more terror for me, another shadow to be explained. That's
why I sat in movie theaters. Because there were no shadows,
only the same blue light. I knew I had to say something.

"I bet." I tried to make my voice sound low and confiding.
The red-haired man's eyes grew and I saw the unlimited,
disparaging blue, the clear hardness of them.

"You're a sport," he said kindly, then yelped, "Goddammit, Ann!"

I could feel the air in back of me where the blond woman
left his wheelchair. I heard her whisper to me, "Thanks,"
then hurry back to her friend.

"I'm so sorry. You could have fallen." Ann grasped the
man and positioned him in his chair. He put his arms on
the armrests with authority, like he was sitting down to a
state dinner, at the head of the table, and everyone was
watching. I saw a tattoo on the top of his head, on his bald

spot. It was a flower with a knife. Two words framed the flower and the knife. They read STILL ALIVE.

The red-haired man turned to his friend in a gesture of comfort.

"Don't worry about me, honey. Guys like me don't fall down. We just go boom." There was momentary laughter, then silence.

I heard my own intake of breath and realized he heard it too. He turned around and stared at me.

"That's what the truth sounds like, mister. You hear it in a dark movie house. You hear it all over the goddamn place and it makes you breathe more than once. That's what it's there for." He spoke to me casually, mocking. Then he turned back to his friend Ann, who was visibly embarrassed.

I was angry and moved to another section of the theater. I heard Ann say, "See, look what you've done." The red-haired man said nothing.

I didn't come to a matinee because I wanted to trade philosophy with a legless Vietnam vet, and I couldn't feel sorry for anyone. I bought my ticket to get out of the August Los Angeles sun, to be in the dark.

There were only three of us at that matinee. During *Indochine* the man spoke in a loud voice and didn't stop.

"That's not Saigon," he intoned over and over. "That's not Saigon."

Catherine Deneuve didn't hear us. She was making love to a younger, feline, tanned man who played a French officer. They were in an abandoned family house, tropical light coming through broken shutters, and there were beads of sweat on their foreheads.

"Just watch the movie, Virgil," his friend Ann muttered.

"Look there. The Vietnamese would never do that. They'd kill first." He said this halfway through the film, lowering his voice to a disgusted monotone.

"This is set in the thirties, Virgil. For God's sake, it's not supposed to be real," Ann said.

"Saigon! Saigon was never real. Don't you see?" The red-haired man crunched up a box of Jordan Almonds and tossed them across the audience, aiming for me.

"No, I don't see," Ann snapped, "and if you don't shut up I swear I will leave you here." I could hear her across the room. She was serious.

"Fuck you," Virgil said without hesitation.

"That's the last movie I take you to." Ann fumbled with her bag and stood up, the smoked, frozen movie light running over her frosted blond hair. "You'll get home just fine, asshole. You always do."

Silence.

I didn't move in my seat. I hoped I would appear invisible, that maybe he would have forgotten I was there. After twenty minutes I heard him speak again, this time to me.

"Don't worry, mister, I won't bite you." His voice was steady.

I thought for a moment, then spoke evenly.

"It certainly is a long film, isn't it?"

This red-haired man, this Virgil with an opinion, seemed relieved.

"I've seen it four times. I keep coming back and I don't know why. I was there. I never liked those Oliver Stone films. Dumb. I don't understand why I am here. Ann's sick and tired of me." His voice crawled out of the shadows and said I dare you. I dare you to take an interest.

"I never saw houses like that in 'seventy. Of course by then everything was blown to hell."

"The French colonials were gone by then," I volunteered. I thought of rows of seats and chasms. Why I sat in empty movie theaters. It was a small movie house. If I were to assign a year for each seat, I would be in a middle row. If I lived long enough, I would be on the screen.

I realized Virgil hadn't replied. Perhaps he was considering what I said.

"Lot of people in Saigon still speak French, but it's a dirty French," he suddenly remarked loudly.

I said nothing.

"Mister, will you help me into my chair when the movie's over?" His voice had become childlike, afraid to beg. "I can't sit here all afternoon. It happened once. The kids with the flashlights forgot all about me." My skin chilled. I was being asked to touch him.

"Of course I will," I said.

"I know what you're thinking," Virgil said distinctly, across the movie house night. I didn't reply. In front of me, Catherine Deneuve was holding a parasol, watching her adopted Chinese daughter marry in an ancient palace slithering with incense and lacquered women.

"You're thinking it will feel strange to touch me. Perhaps a flap of flesh will hit you. Or something not right, something healed and ugly. A contamination or some kind of radiation. None of that's true. I'm soft as a baby's bottom, mister."

His voice was almost happy. I thought of serial killers and how normal they become after each kill.

"I wasn't thinking that at all," I stuttered. My shoulders had become hot.

"Watch the movie," Virgil said sweetly. "It gets real dramatic from here on in."

Outside the theater I knew I was trapped.

"Will you drive me home? Please, mister. It's a hundred and one and I'm not flush for a cab. It'd be the bus and the sun." Virgil looked up at me through his sunglasses.

I was not ready to stumble. To take on things I didn't understand.

"All right," I said.

This I remember. The sun was livid, incontinent with heat. I began to push Virgil's wheelchair.

"Great. You can come to my house in Canoga Park. I got a big air conditioner, biggest and best in town. I'll fix you iced tea or something. I know you don't drink." Virgil brought out a tiny black notepad from the pocket of his shorts and wrote something I couldn't see.

"How do you know?" I wondered.

"You look it," he answered.

Our friendship began like this. At a movie house. And it stayed this way for two years. We were not particularly fond of one another as friends. We did not celebrate our birthdays or talk about personal things. No Christmas cards. We went to movies twice a week for those two years. Virgil's friend Ann didn't come back.

I didn't mind helping him with his wheelchair, lifting him.

He had very muscular arms. One afternoon I caught myself thinking what he would be like with legs. I had to stand in the theater lobby for ten minutes and breathe, look at the sun through the glass doors. Anything. Virgil didn't notice, and handed me a box of frozen Butterfingers when I came back in.

I wanted to know about Virgil's Saigon. He liked to tell me, and I listened. Being almost alone in my life was like a magic made from razors. It had to be bled once, twice a week, and I bled it with Virgil, at movies, at Mexican restaurants like Casa Vega, full of leftover rock and rollers, where the light was so dim the waitress carried a flashlight.

Virgil wore a stainless steel Timex watch whose face was so scratched I couldn't see its time, and he said that's exactly why he wore it. To ask strangers what time it was. To see if they were still bound to days and months and noons.

He had a deep, powdery voice, a midwestern boy's voice, on the verge of a twang but ready for escape. This kind of voice doesn't change into manhood, and didn't for Virgil. It resonates a belief in all things far away, of seeing the unattainable.

Chewing on his taco, Virgil told me that when bits of his leg were tossed out of an army helicopter's doors into the red water of the China Sea, he had finally seen the unattainable. He said it was a lurid white nowhere, and he could feel a malice pumping into his chest, not self-created, but a being that sat with him on the flight, cackling.

He mentioned smoke and the nurse's perfume, a solid wax made from Hawaiian plumeria, and sold in Singapore in mother of pearl shells. It was on her thumbs as she injected him.

When the morphine finally kicked in, a tape deck was playing "Hot Fun in the Summertime" by Sly and the Family Stone. Virgil remembered the images before death and they were not of his family. They were of a thirteen-year-old Vietnamese girl named Linda who kept her beginning pubis shaved to look even younger, and who told him he would return to Saigon to stay.

Ann was long gone, Virgil explained, because she got married. Besides, she was only a volunteer from the DAV.

"A girl like that helps a crip once in her life, to make herself feel good. Then it's shopping and fucking and babies. She calls once a month to see how I am. Did you know that?"

"No," I answered.

Virgil sighed. "She knew I wanted to go to bed with her."

"Did you?" I asked casually. This was new territory. We were at a one o'clock show of *Cliffhanger* with Sylvester Stallone. Virgil was in a quiet mood. We watched a woman fall thousands of feet into a crevice in the Alps.

"She's a goner," Virgil muttered.

I turned and looked at him. He wasn't watching the film.

I offered him some Raisinettes, which he threw in his mouth. He turned his attention back to Stallone.

"This guy's not that hot, and besides, he's getting too old for all this action adventure stuff. I should write a screenplay about Saigon. Then you'd really see something." Virgil knew I was writing a screenplay and he nudged me.

"You want to make big money?" he whispered.

"Sure, Virgil." I tried to cut him off.

"With me it would be. I've seen things you never will."

"You're right, Virgil. I've seen nothing. Let's finish the film." I felt like I had punched myself in the stomach. I sounded like a married woman, agreeing with her husband to shut him up.

"You know, that's your problem. You never want to talk. You got no personality. I've seen it all. You need to come out of your coffin, buddy. Take a look around," Virgil whispered.

I turned and looked at him. His eyes stayed on Stallone. He shook his head, disgusted. I wanted to say, "Virgil, do you know what it's like to be alone because you have to be, because all your friends are dead?" And I realized he would only turn and look at me and say, "Yes. I know all about it."

Virgil didn't know I wrote about Saigon but kept it filed away because when I tried to describe the city it became wooden. The only time it came alive was on Virgil's tongue.

We drank through the afternoon at my apartment. I learned to keep bourbon for Virgil. I was pleased I could keep a bottle of bourbon in my apartment and not drink. It made me feel strong. I listened, saying little, and drove Virgil home when he began to get drunk or tired.

That day I opened the curtains and we looked out my sliding glass doors, onto the pool of my apartment complex. An almost old woman was sitting by the pool with a radio, sunblock, and a one-piece, heavy floral bathing suit with the straps pulled down.

Virgil was watching her too. She was wearing a bright yellow turban and it was electric in the afternoon sun. Frank Sinatra was singing "King of the Road" on her radio. A crow hopped down in back of her and finished the rest of her sandwich. The San Fernando Valley was full of crows.

There was a gold and diamond Star of David around her neck and I looked at it in the sun. I saw a momentary white glimmer that blinded, a faraway blindness, and I turned to speak to Virgil. He stared back at me curiously.

"I meant what I said about Saigon. We could write a movie. And clean up." Virgil grimaced, rubbing his left arm.

I sat down.

"Tell me about Saigon." I said this quietly, knowing Virgil would talk for perhaps an hour. This was our connection, and I understood these afternoons. I was able to weave in and out of war privately, a voyeur and a thief, and I came out with nothing. It was the temperance of a quiet reserved for those who cling, and have little choice. Virgil spoke quietly but with passion. He liked to face the window. He said he had to be able to see things move around in order to remember. His hands tapped the table and he began to speak.

"I lost my virginity in Saigon, to a thirteen-year-old whore named Linda who brought me chicken chow mein with opium in it when I was sick. I had the flu. A horrible thing in Saigon. She didn't care that I was sick and she made love to me until I passed out. I was in love with her and a little Vietnamese boy named Jim. He gave good head. He was ten. We were all good men, American men, oh God, we were eighteen, we were boys. But in Saigon you don't care how you do it as long as you do it." Virgil turned to me.

I lit a cigarette. I didn't know this about Virgil.

"Go on," I said.

"There were colors that stood for things. Like yellow, the brightest yellows, and pinks and oranges and reds. They had meanings only the Vietnamese knew, things never told us. Death, sex, evil, religion, fertility. I saw a Vietnamese man back away from a yellow mask and begin to tear his hair out, on his knees, and we just laughed. We were fresh out of high school in Peoria, and stoned on acid and heroin and an incredible cocaine from Thailand."

Virgil took a sip of bourbon. I closed my eyes for a moment, to walk into his dream, to pretend my life had vanished, that I was no longer lonely, or afraid, or desperate. Virgil continued.

"I remember seeing a beautiful building with a wrought-iron balcony, just like the ones you see in the French Quarter in New Orleans, you know, the postcard ones, and I thought there should be whores hanging out, in lacy dresses, waving to the soldiers from those balconies. I closed my eyes then opened them and they were there, with Chinese fans and G-strings and high heels, with lace curtains blowing in hot air, and I learned all you have to do in Saigon is imagine what you want and it comes to you right away. If you want to kill a man, you take out a gun and shoot anyone in the street and it's cool. A few people scream, and then it's just another dead person on the sidewalk, with bicycle tracks on his heels. Anything you want, it's there. You understand?"

I nodded my head and opened my eyes. Virgil watched the pool lady get up, pull up her straps and wade into the pool and submerge herself to her shoulders, bouncing lightly. Then she started to do little kicks in the shallow end. Virgil licked his lips and gently rubbed his scalp.

"I did that once to prove I could kill for no reason at all. I had scored some serious crank and I was flying, the same flight you get when you dream, and I wasn't so sure I wasn't dreaming so I figured if I shot someone that would be proof enough. You know, touch the wound, smell the blood. Then I would know I was still going. Still alive, and not dreaming. I pulled out my gun a half an hour later, on a crowded street where they sold fish from the China Sea, bad diseased fish you couldn't eat, and I shot an old man in the head. He was on a bike. He fell. I reached down and put my palm on his wound. It was pulsing and very hot. I was elated. I picked up his bike. People were screaming, running for cover. I rode away singing a Stones' tune. It was great."

I stubbed my cigarette out.

"I didn't know you liked to kill," I said hesitantly.

"I was going on nineteen. It was a war. I was stoned. I got no regrets. In Saigon you smoke a little opium and you either lay down in a den or you walk the streets. If you walk the streets you see things flying that aren't really there. You see giant butterflies and birds made of jade and warplanes, bombers that look like silver wasps. You see girls with gold teeth and tiny brown nipples. They all have American names like Judy and Linda and Sally and Liz, Liz was big, lots of girls named Liz. And every day is young, tropical, thirsty, sexual. I woke up to blood, I killed a lot of people. I stole and ate everything and wound up sick. That's why you take the dope, to keep the death away. And it stays away."

Virgil wheeled himself over to the bar and poured himself another bourbon. Then he positioned himself in front of the window and sipped.

"There's more. See, there's always more in Saigon. Did I ever tell you how the city smelled like a giant magnolia at night and like a corpse during the day? Places where they buried the dead, the nameless places where they dug a hole big enough to fit twelve or fourteen, behind a house or a restaurant or a market, then cover the bodies with lye and beer and go on and forget, walk down the street, and the sun would hit and you'd know: Oh boy would you know. And you didn't care. I didn't care."

I realized I was terrified. And elated. And that my expression, or my lack of, hadn't changed. I couldn't let him see my hand flutter the wrong way, or a lisp come to my tongue. I was on the inside, looking out. Still observing, emotionless. Lousy.

"I was completely alive and I was going to live forever and I knew it. That's why they have the young fight wars. Because old men are too crafty, too sly, too comfortable. This is a once in a lifetime gig, man. It doesn't happen again, and I was there, and I was young. I saw Buddhas being carted away that were made of solid amethyst, can you dig it? Everywhere red and gold, then fire and char. Have you ever caught the fragrance of napalm? Well, not in Saigon but twenty kilometers north? It smells like the perfumed devil. It smells like the wrong whore. The whore with a knife under her pillow."

Virgil was silent as the woman got out of the pool and dried herself off with a pink towel, then calmly leaned back into her chaise lounge.

"When I found out my legs were gone . . ." He lost his concentration and stared at me.

"I've known you two years. You're homosexual, aren't you?" Virgil asked this so quickly my mouth twitched.

"Yes," I answered. "And?"

"You act real wifey around me. Guys don't do that. I don't care. I'm going to call you wifey."

I suddenly thought of someone who discovers a suicide. The white light, the horror and the head-shaking, the backing away. Something has been stolen. I realized Virgil was studying me.

"Don't you have a boyfriend?" He asked innocently.

"No." My voice sounded high-pitched and strained.

"Well, I mean. You're good-looking. Your hair is clean."

I composed myself.

"It's very dangerous today, Virgil."

"No shit. Just like Saigon. You know, Los Angeles. The warriors are born every decade and they're here. And they're young. Gangs. Assholes. I've seen them. They won't bother me. I'm just half a kill. But the perfumed devil is here." His tone had become belligerent. I knew he was getting tired, and a little drunk. Soon I would drive him home.

I walked over to his wheelchair to see if he needed to go to the bathroom. He grabbed my arm and looked up at me.

"I watch. That's how I do it. I watch. I never stop watching. I pay for it and I watch." Virgil's tone was melancholic. "I'm not queer. That's what you do too. Watch."

From Virgil, I wanted war, tropical mornings, Chinese whores, planes. I wanted to stay within the frame of our private films, the film on Virgil's tongue. I wanted Virgil to stay, unchanged, in front of my poolside window. A man I could show to the world, without disease, safe as a song in church. Neighbors would nod their heads knowingly and say, Ah, he's not alone anymore.

"I don't like to watch. I don't. I'm not a pervert, man. It's all . . . my testicles were removed when my legs were removed."

The air became rigid and hollow. I watched Virgil. His

eyes had turned pink as the woman's towel outside, but not moist. I could hear Ella Fitzgerald sing "Mack the Knife" outside, on the radio. The woman was busy smearing suntan lotion on with deliberate jabs on her shoulders.

I continued to watch Virgil. "Yes, Virgil. I'm queer. I'm alone." My words surprised me.

"I tell you what, you take me into your bedroom and you do it for me, I want to see you. If you don't understand me, understand I ain't looking at you. I'm looking at everything young, pulsing with blood and life, nothing maimed or damaged."

I began to laugh.

"I have AIDS, Virgil. Do you want to talk about damaged goods? You've seen the medicines by my bed, the IV stand, for God's sake?"

"Oh, I knew you had AIDS when we first met."

Silence.

"How? How did you know?"

"When a man gets this look, you see it on soldiers who've just been shot, you see it on guys running into the jungle with guns on their back, it's a look that's taking in everything and everything's really alive, bright as hell, brightest in your life, and you're running with Death holding your hand."

I had to sit down, and breathe very slowly.

"So, I told you the truth. It's a dose, never pretty. So whaddya say you go in there and show me what kind of man you are. All my ghosts will be watching you. All the little exotics, the Lindas. They'll be clapping their hands."

I got up from my chair, looked at Virgil, and walked into the bedroom. As I unbuttoned my shirt I could hear the electric motor of Virgil's wheelchair dinging as he approached the bedroom door.

"I just want to remember, that's all," Virgil whispered.

I saw Virgil one other time, and it was the last. I was at LAX, at the China Airlines terminal. Virgil had called to tell me he was taking a trip. Would I come to see him off? I asked where. He said Saigon, where else?

It was the middle of June and the morning was overcast, carrying the salt of the Pacific in its crusted edge, and the low clouds hadn't cleared. The light washing the terminal was a distinct pearl color, softening the room and making people's hair and skin glimmer. It had the unreality of any dream not remembered, and I found it difficult to breathe.

I had not spoken to Virgil for several months. Virgil called watching me masturbate "a mercy fuck; but a needed one." We realized there were no more movies to see.

There were many Chinese and Vietnamese families getting ready to board the plane. They wore Rodeo Drive T-shirts and pressed jeans. I wondered where they were headed. If they were just going to Hawaii or anywhere still safe and rich and mindless, where there are no warriors, or perfumed devils. These people were not refugees. They sat and stood too easily. They didn't have food, or the traces of food in their hands. They had already eaten.

Suddenly I noticed white American men, clustered in packs through the crowd like friendly animals at a petting zoo. Some of these men were blind. Some had claws for hands, others had parts of their hands covered with rings and tattoos. Many were paraplegic. Several used walkers. Then I saw men not maimed, but bloated, with deeply tanned faces and crew cuts. One threw an airline bottle of vodka into an ashtray and immediately opened another, taking small sips as he walked to the check-in desk.

Every man here was middle-aged. Every man was happy. They were part of the group Virgil mentioned hurriedly over the phone. They had fought in Vietnam and they were going to Saigon on vacation. And some of them, Virgil explained, bought one-way tickets.

I saw Virgil sitting near a window. His carry-on luggage was positioned on his lap. He was wearing short shorts and I could see his stumps. He did this on purpose. He wanted everyone to see them today.

Virgil waved me over, smiling. Ann was sitting behind him, holding a toddler and not smiling. I came up to Virgil and shook his hand.

"Send me a postcard, Virgil. I want to see what Saigon looks like," I said.

Virgil laughed.

"I'll send you ten. But the mail sucks in Southeast Asia, friend, and you already know what it looks like."

"Yes," I murmured.

An airline attendant asked Virgil his name and checked it off on a list, then took his wheelchair and began to wheel him to the boarding ramp. We followed. Virgil couldn't stop talking.

"They serve ice cold beer on silver trays now, that's what I hear. And shrimp with mint and chili. Since the war a black orchid, real rare, now grows everywhere. The whores pin them in their hair for luck."

"All the little Lindas?" I ask, almost sweetly. Virgil studied me.

"Yeah, stud, the May Lings and Suzies in black leather and sunglasses from Paris. And all the little Lindas, singing in a chorus, saying welcome home, Virgil, 'We love you, baby,' in that chink squeak, and I'll be sitting on coconut palms on China Beach with a servant girl." Then Virgil winked at me.

"Maybe a servant boy too. But Ann looks tired. Ann always is kind of tired."

Virgil muttered an uncomfortable goodbye to Ann and she muttered goodbye back. Then he asked me to bend down so he could whisper in my ear.

"You were good, wifey, real good. A sport. But sooner or later you got to rock and roll. Or you die. I'm not coming back. Saigon's the best. The fucking best. The best city of all time."

I wanted to say, "Virgil, look, I've lifted you and been your friend. I've let you watch me come in a darkened room because you begged me, and I remember there were tears in your eyes after my last spasm and shudder, and you couldn't swallow. Only whisper 'Take me home.' I haven't had a drink in two years, seen over a hundred action adventure films with you. I hate action pictures."

I held back. Ann came up to me. Her child, a little boy, was asleep against her chest, a tiny string of drool staining her blouse. She had no makeup on. She studied me.

"I remember you," she said. "You're the guy who took my place." Ann didn't smile. She turned her gaze away from me and watched Virgil in line. "I miss going to the movies. There's just no time."

Ann quietly hoisted her child up against her hip. He

squirmed, opened his eyes to look at me, then fell back asleep.

"Virgil's an asshole," Ann said, and walked away.

I began to cry, a girlish cry, embarrassed at my tears. The morning gray lifted into a smothering, white-hot Los Angeles sun. Suddenly conversation increased in volume, goodbyes were being said, omens accepted. Virgil began to disappear into that lurid white nowhere, chatting with a man who used a walker like he was jumping rope. I wiped my eyes and tried to catch Virgil's words as he disappeared into the on-ramp tunnel.

He always had pronounced the words Vietnam, Saigon, Cochin, and the Mouths of the Mekong, the Islands Les Deux Freres, Bong Son, Goc Thrang, and Phan Rang as though they were chants in a prayer. Or the slow *om* Buddhists use to clear their heads for visions. He often joked that when the Mouths of the Mekong ate his legs, they burped, and he could hear it across the Mekong Delta.

That's Vietnam, Virgil intoned. Always hungry. Rice fields everywhere and still the land was hungry, the rivers, beaches, those bizarre mountains, the jungles. All of them hungry for blood, souls, meat. I can't explain it, Virgil whispered. It just is.

vaudeville

Linda Gomez adjusts her District Attorney's sensible battleship-gray Italian leather high heels and thinks, God. I want to put my feet in the sand at the beach. Near the old roller coaster on Pacific Beach. I don't care if the water's cold. I don't care if my feet turn that light shade of blue I see on asphyxiations at the city morgue. I want my ankles immersed in fluid sand.

"Listen to this tape," Allison says in a hushed voice. Allison is Linda's assistant and is quite competent, but Linda doesn't like Allison's perkiness, her cheerful young clean face, the way she nods and smiles like a marionette.

Linda has always hoped Allison has some sort of secret, pornographic agenda. To put a down payment on her condo at La Jolla Shores, Allison works as a dominatrix, or better yet, as a nude dancer at the Mile High Club in Tijuana. On Sunday afternoon. After church.

A pornographic agenda is what every woman needs, Linda thinks. A slow slide into something completely without remorse, requiring body fluids, dark rooms, and a new personality.

Then the caricature of a life, a return to efficiency. When Linda Gomez found out her husband of twelve years had not one but three mistresses, in Tijuana, she only wanted to know their names, these afternoon border girls with children and shoes from Saks Fifth Avenue. The private detective she hired was a woman with an overtly muscular body, dyed blond hair, and an obscene amount of energy. Celine was her name. Linda remembers cringing upon hearing that name, then cringing even more when the mistresses' names came up. Angelica, Maria Magdalena, Esther.

A triad of angels, Linda thinks. She wonders if they go to church and pray. Linda is amused, thinks they tell the priest nothing and never have. Linda imagines them assuming a new persona for each man, always telling them you're the only man in my life. I'm so lonely. Leave your wife for me. Give my child a father. Help me.

"Altogether we're looking at five, possibly six murders, all of them infants, children under the ages of four. Both sexes." This is Lew's voice. Linda likes Lew. He is two months away from forty, well-built, wears suits from Sears. Lew has four children and a wife named Heather, who once confided to Linda at a Christmas function that Lew "was the best lay in San Diego. Like a baseball bat, honey. A home run every night."

"Run the tape," Linda says, looking out the window. Below her the huge, floating bridge crossing San Diego Bay to Coronado is fairly free of cars. But it is always fairly free of cars, Linda thinks. Like everything in San Diego. Fairly free of cars. Fairly good food. Fairly warm weather.

"Here's her picture." Allison hands Linda a photograph taken yesterday at police headquarters. It shows a woman with a wizened face and stringy reddish-blond hair. At first Linda thinks the parched look must be from the sun, but then she looks closer. The woman looks like a methamphetamine freak, Linda reasons. Looks like you could snap your fingers and she'd put her hands to her ears from the noise.

The tape begins. The woman's voice is stretched, reedy.

"It's not like I didn't love them. It was the noise I couldn't handle. . . . They were so naughty." Linda stops the tape.

"Put down methamphetamine," Linda says to Lew, who nods, sipping his coffee. Lew is never surprised by anything. Linda likes that. She turns the tape back on, then fast forwards it.

"Bill and I were in Scranton. We decided to be Mr. and Mrs. Cupper from Toledo. I put on a little lime-green dress I bought at a thrift shop, sensible shoes like a housewife would wear. Even some pearls from Woolworth's. We decided to knock on the first door on this one street, and say we just moved into the neighborhood. . . ."

Linda understands how lies can be kind. Even from killers. The dying and the soon to be dead, everyone wants a story. Everyone wants an entertainment.

She remembers how she always made sure she smiled at her husband, and kept her eyes crinkly, charming. All those years of telling him, in their brightly lit, white furniture world, that he was the finest man she knew. All the dinner parties for business associates who stole his money. All his relatives with children who broke her china.

Let's see, who have I been recently? Linda thinks. As many women as I can. I'm the bitch who signs the checks.

I'm the forgotten wife, the childless whore, the woman at a high-rise window, staring intently at the same scene.

She can see the bare outline of the Hotel del Coronado with its spires and rotting, salted wood. Linda thinks, This is where my husband and I will have dinner tonight. That way I will be able to walk on the beach. A cool, moonlit wind and low tide. No shoes.

"Once inside, they were easy to kill. One old lady had tons of money all over the house. And her granddaughter. This cute little baby. So I took it." The tape is stopped.

"I'll go and get lunch," Allison says in a teary voice, rising quickly and doing her little bunny hop to the door. Lew adjusts his long frame in the leather club chair. He turns the tape back on as Linda turns back to the window.

It is noon, and Linda sees the fairly hazy noontime glare that descends on the city once the fog burns off. She puts on her sunglasses, normally on top of her head. No squinting. No laugh lines. The fog, deep and rich and always perfumed, is the only thing Linda loves about San Diego.

There are things a woman can do in a dense fog, Linda reasons. Put on a new dress and get in a car, find a motel, a room with hibiscus draperies and forty watt bulbs, a place where the fog never lifts. Leave the door open, the lights on, and screw any man who walks through the door. Listen to the foghorns and booming heaves of navy ships docking in the bay. Wear a bra with holes cut out for her nipples.

Linda is tired of the third act. It is an exceptionally long third act. She is ready to serve divorce papers, but keeps hoping her husband will change, that a new song will perhaps enter their lives, one where the dance steps are easy.

Listening to the tape, she crosses her arms and yawns,

thinking what she will order tonight. A grilled lobster salad
with jicama. She will have a sensible white wine, one from
Northern California, with a fairly decent bouquet. Her husband will repeat the same conversation they have on their
"special" dinner nights:

"You don't seem to enjoy our life together anymore."

"I told you. I deal with death and cruelty. Horror every
day."

"It pays well."

"That it does."

They will raise their glasses and toast. The candlelight will
be soft, flickering. Linda will get fairly tight, but not drunk,
and her husband will laugh his young man's laugh, and say,
"There's my girl. You want to walk on the beach? Sure,
we'll walk on the beach."

"I didn't want to kill anybody, honest I didn't, but Bill
liked to be on the road. I always wanted a kid, but every
time we took a cute one, it always seemed to get in the way.
Bill would get mad at all the crying."

"What about Bill?" Linda asks Lew as she stops the tape.

"Apparently he worked as a clown in some low-end cir-
cuses, mostly midwestern outfits. No criminal record prior
to meeting her."

"So they were bad news together," Linda thinks aloud.

"Probably kept the sex hot," Lew says noncommittally.

"Probably. Figure drugs, speed, meth, anything to keep
them on the silver highway. Then sexual passion. Blood becomes exciting."

"The kids?"

Linda shakes her head. She is not certain. She motions from the window for Lew to put the tape back on.

At this moment she sees, from the eighteenth floor, a Goodyear blimp slowly bludgeoning its way across the Southern California sky. Linda is pleased to see it, remembers it from last month. It will advertise a suntan lotion from Hawaii in electric lights that repeat every two minutes. If the blimp is up and about, she thinks, then by the end of the afternoon there will be a skywriter or two, planes twisting with white smoke, writing, "Happy Anniversary Jo-Ann" or "Catch the wave on KFKT, your beach FM."

Linda knows a child will point up to the sky in wonder, sitting on a lap, and an adult voice will say, "It's not that big of a deal. It happens all the time."

Suddenly she remembers her last dinner, on Tuesday night, with her husband. She had made her excuses, and he had made his. They had shared a chocolate dessert with truffles. The waiter knew them by name.

"Perhaps we should use fantasy," her husband suggested.

"A different part every Saturday night?" Linda intimated, arching one eyebrow.

"Perhaps. Well, not every week, but every once in a while."

"I see. Sort of changing the act on the bill every week? What happens if the act is perfectly good? Two curtain calls a night?"

"Don't be so complacent, Linda. Old acts, same music. That's how vaudeville died."

Linda's mouth dropped open. She began to laugh, irritating her husband, who rose to leave, handing her her cashmere shawl. All he could do was mutter about an early morning flight. Motherfucker, Linda thought that evening, driving home to Torrey Pines, her husband asleep in the passenger seat. You son of a bitch cocksucker. You fifty-year-old failure.

"Sorry. Play that last bit, where she talks about her clothes," Linda says to Lew. She is warm now, standing next to the window. The sun feels good.

"See, when we were on the road, it's like I could be any-one, anything. For a while I kept that lime-green dress from Scranton, then I wore a tweed skirt and pointy glasses. Bill told everyone I was a librarian. I mean, sure, we killed a lot of old ladies on the road. But let's face it, they were ready to go, and we needed the money. 'Sides, Bill and I met a lot of nice couples on the road. There was Ray and Anita. I'd always send Anita a postcard wherever we was. Anita gave me a whole bag of makeup from Revlon. One night I got dressed up as a hooker, just for Bill. We really partied that night. It was at a motel in Yuma. I put on a blond wig, like Marilyn Monroe. It was real hot that night. Then I got in the pool naked and lifted one leg over the side, you know, just like Marilyn in that pool, right before she died, with that real surprised look on her face? Bill took pictures. Boy, did we laugh. I remember there were thousands of stars in the sky that night. And I remember my face was covered with this thin layer of sand the next morning. See, there are white, white sand dunes all 'round Yuma, and they blow all the time. Always changing around."

Linda tries to remember when she first started visiting that motel, in the fog. It felt good, all the different men. The different shapes of penises, some fat and sloppy, others hard and short. She was always amused at how easy it was, how they came so quickly, how she said "shhh" and put one finger to her lips when they asked her name.

No money, she thinks, and smiles. I was never a whore at that motel. It was the embrace, the body hair, a man's breath believing my breasts were his for the moment.

She watched a hundred girls like the one on the tape stay the night, at that motel, scarred by losers and still believing in the magic of the open road. Girls with two years to live. Girls with ten dollars in their panties and a purse full of speed and cigarettes. Girls who lose children in motel rooms in New Mexico, not waking up in Arizona or Nevada. Not waking up, ever.

This is why I have no heart, Linda thinks. I've screwed on the beds of lost children and dead women and it is my secret. My husband's secrets I know, and he knows absolutely zero about me. Silly old ham. Has-been.

"Fast forward," Linda says as Allison bounces in with lunch. Six chicken tacos, two veggie burritos, and a cucumber salad. How utterly vile, Linda thinks, starting on her veggie burrito with a plastic fork. Linda nods, her mouth full. The tape begins again.

"I don't know where Bill is and I ain't lyin'. I remember we had this little boy, maybe two years old, we got in St. Louis, and he was cute as a button, a towhead. But Bill was feeling really low and we were two days without a stash. The kid started yelling, so Bill put him under a cushion on the sofa and sat on top of him until the hollering stopped. We were at the Golden Sky Motel in Idaho. I still got the matches, I always collect the matches, that's how I remember. Bill tells me to get rid of the kid so I put him in a suitcase and walked him down to the All-Nite Mart, where they had one of those great big trash cans.''

"Jesus Christ," Lew says. He is crying. His head is in his hands.

"Take a break, Lew. I'll continue," Linda says quietly. "You better go too, Allison. Work for a while on the water rights papers."

Allison and Lew silently leave, relieved. Linda knows her reputation. That nothing ever gets to her. She turns the tape back on, watching the sun glitter and polish the roofs and highways of a fairly nice seaside city.

"When I got back to the room Bill had cleared out. I sorta expected him to, 'cause we didn't have much exciting with each other anymore. In a sort of crazy way, I always felt we were kind of in show biz, you know? New personality, new act. We used to sit up all night, good and cranked, and think up new characters. One time we were the Smiths, a couple from Phoenix, another time we were a brother and sister. The brother was supposed to be deaf, so I had to interpret. I didn't know sign language, 'course no one else did either, so I pretended. Worked like a charm. We got in the house. An old bitch with a hearing aid!''

Linda Gomez continues to listen to the tape. She finishes her burrito and pours herself a Diet Coke. She locks the door to her office and takes off her shoes, wiggling her toes.

"You guys'll never find Bill. He's somebody else now. I probably wouldn't know him. See, Bill's a barbarian, a genius. We don't need anything. We're the new breed. We're everywhere. Why be a mother once when I can be a mother six times? And I can always move on. I'm still young and pretty. I'm twenty-five years old. I'm still filled with love, baby. I'm free as a bird and I'm like no one else. Don't you get it? Don't you guys fucking get it?"

Linda presses her finger on the tape machine's stop button. Suddenly her office is dead silent. No phones ring. She can even hear the air-conditioning turn on.

I'm still young and pretty, Linda thinks. I got no kids. I'll divorce my husband, move to Paris, marry a prince. I'm still filled with love and free as a bird.

She makes some mental notes. The girl on the tape is beyond rehabilitation. Go for the death penalty. If there are problems at the State Supreme Court, plea bargain for life imprisonment without the possibility of parole. Don't take calls from any of the families of the victims.

The afternoon sun has made her office very warm, bleaching it to a bareness Linda likes. She is swimming in a white, warm sea. She loosens her neck scarf and gold and lapis brooch. She runs her hand through her straight black hair. She opens her handbag and touches up her face, then looks through her appointment book.

She makes a reservation at the Del Coronado for two, for dinner, and the maitre d' says cheerfully over the phone, "Oh, Mr. and Mrs. Gomez, we always love having you and your husband. Thursday evenings are always fun with you and Mr. Gomez. I'll chill your favorite wine," and suddenly Linda is aware of a tiny, deep voice coming from below her larynx. Swirling in tired breath, it says, "Don't you get it? Don't you guys fucking well get it?"

iguana boy

Everything starts with a postcard, Evangeline thinks. It is an emblem of transience, a fast, unburdened thought sent with a picture both foreign and injected with the same severe color as dreams. There are implications of people who love differently, with unusual skin and language, breathing air that carries disease only they fall from. Travelers are protected by God and shielded by their own temporary glamour.

Certain postcards become magic. Like the one that brushed up to her feet today, scraping against her heel, saying bend down old woman, pick me up, forget your life. I come to you through circumstances. I am free and mysterious. You can throw me away if you don't like my piece of earth, my blue mountains. My sun and sky.

Evangeline is eighty years old and sits with a straw hat in the sun of her cement backyard, which isn't even a backyard but an animal pen, a kennel missing doors. Here she has painted walls peach and green, but pots of mint and bulbs in even rows on each side of the chain-link gate. She has a small writing table and chair that sits outside, often in the rain, so it becomes cozy and weathered. When the Los Angeles sun is clear and yellow-white, Evangeline sits at her table so she can feel she is in the south of France, or Cairo, or Beirut twenty years ago, writing postcards to her friends around the world. Evangeline has no friends. They have all died, or have slid into infirmity, their faces leering with paralysis, their conversations nasty and taxing.

Evangeline will have none of it. She knows solitude comes like a friend before death, but she is not ready to stop, become inconsequential or delicate. There is still the sky and sea, and other cities she hasn't seen. The sky has watched her pick this postcard up, in the garbage of her East Hollywood street, and said nothing. Sometimes it speaks, and Evangeline listens, waiting for it to wash its foreign air over her arms.

People. The smell of food cooked in markets. Women with kohl eyes and gold teeth, their breasts soaked in cinnamon and rose water, somehow cool under black cloth and screaming like parrots in the Yucatan, coins clenched in their toes. Jamaica. Mecca. Madrid. Buenos Aires. Sometimes this air comes in spurts into her cement garden, carrying voices still trapped in their own scent, drifting like a questioned dust in front of her.

Everything worthwhile is an act of the imagination. A hard lesson perhaps, but Evangeline knows, after eighty years, that reality is on the corner, under a palm or an olive tree, waiting to cross a street, any street that's busy and ignorant. It walks her street, calling for her like a young man in a state of heat, and she keeps her door locked, candles lit, and her legs crossed.

She is rubbing the postcard between her fingers. Soon she will read it. She used to love receiving postcards, thinking part of her is sitting under a hotel desk. An old hotel, not one frequented by tourists, but by travelers, people who never cease moving through cities and drinking them like local alcohol, people who never have luggage or reasons or families.

And one of these travelers, with eyes full of Caribbean ten cent rum and the sleep that follows revolutions, would be writing to her. Somewhere, these visitors are lonely, frightened of people who do not see them or understand what they say. And these travelers are thinking of Evangeline. Just the idea she is being thought of in a foreign place gives her power. Her spirit is walking around the world.

She has planned many trips and given up on all of them. She has kept many scrapbooks of each trip, carefully cutting pictures out of color brochures and pasting them in her books. In notes she writes beside each picture, she never lies. Evangeline is very careful to annotate with simple facts, never giving anything away.

When she writes, "This is the Grand Hotel, Rome" next to a picture of the Grand Hotel, there is certainly no denying it. What she is really writing to herself is "This is where I stayed, oblivious to the heat that circled Rome like a witch. I remember the chandelier in my room had ice blue Czechoslovakian crystals that were cracked by age and the cage of the electric bulb. I remember hearing cats in the Villa Borghese, smelling orange blossoms out of season. I remember the man in the next room was beating his wife, then making love to her, then crying on his balcony just before dawn, and I listened, listened for my life, and these are the jewels

I carry with me, the objects I display on shelves." Evangeline knows after her death someone will go through these books and be impressed by her range of travels, her taste in selecting such lovely pictures (assuming she didn't like to photograph things), and her ability for detail. They will never see the invisible ink, the supposition that keeps her alive.

Evangeline can't travel because she is poor, and has always been poor. She has never stopped educating herself to someday assume a comfortable place in the world, but it hasn't happened. On her television she sees ads for a perfume called Escape and listens by instinct, knowing to escape is to redefine a landscape, but to travel is much more.

She wishes she could travel the way rich widows do, women with beige wool that never creases and alligator heels, who walk alone on ships and check off the places they still haven't seen. She knows them. She knows how they evaporate with each breath. When she was young, she was pretty. It could have happened to her. She has passed by these women on occasion and smelled the powder, cigarettes, and men. These are the women who meet for tea in Cairo, under ceiling fans in rooms crawling with ancient mosaics, the smell of chalk and honey, their passports encased in polished burgundy leather, their lipstick carefully applied to match the color of sunsets.

They remark on their daughters and sons, the correct agenda and way to travel. Like which fine hotels still have tissue-thin stationery with gold embossing. Or the best bargains in Singapore, down streets shuddering with plaque, and children with flies in their hair, where gold and sapphires from Bangkok can be had for nothing.

Every year a new city goes into her books. She is careful

to pick only the most exciting and opulent. The brochures are always easy to find. She hunts in trash cans behind travel agencies and rent-a-car firms. She has discovered Bali and Puerto Rico and Maui, touching down long enough for those rich widows and ceaseless travelers who make up her dream to be aware that someone is beside them. Something transparent, keen and alert for sensation. I close my eyes and sit in my chair, here in the sun, and I'm there.

They are listening to me, Evangeline thinks. They hear me when they are caught off guard, somewhere they are unfamiliar with. They feel me behind them when they are exiting a plane into a tropical heat scented with magnolia and shellfish. I am tapping their shoulder, murmuring I am here with you, and they turn, palms and ocean behind them like slow dancers at the end of a night. Their faces ask who, what, and gasoline fumes smother the airport pavement. They see nothing at all, their faces framed like a postcard, and they descend the painted metal stairs into the noise, the sugar of a new destination. The picture hardens to a sheen.

She is able to remember her dreams. I have been to Maui, Evangeline whispers to herself. I've seen its random grace of hideous yellows, and sugarcane fields that slither like chiffon on a whore. I have slept there in an undertow of plumeria blossoms and Kona storms and I will return. I have been to every beautiful, hot place, and they are all worth visiting twice. Here I can be of a certain age, dressed in perfect cottons and walking beside these rich widows, and gigolos and criminals and everyone alone, passing through, their skin smooth from new cities a week at a time. I am traveling beyond all the lives I could have had, or had presented to me by fate, and I am fast as smoke, smart, and embarking for distances and different lights.

The Indian summer sun speaks the same language as the sky. Today it says do not look at me, Evangeline. I'll burn you into someone else, an unfamiliar. Stick to your sun hat and your painted dog kennel. Your travels on postcards and brochures are meaningless. Lose hope, trust no one, as no one trusts you. I am old age. I am your future. I am the marble you found yesterday, covered with the grease of children's fingers. If you look past the chips you will see my eye.

She stares at this postcard she found on the street. Evangeline feels she has stolen it but she does not feel guilty. It blew up to her feet. On purpose. The tiny cottage she lives in is only six feet from the street, and the owners cemented all its lawn and shrubbery to cut down on maintenance. Evangeline notices the most beautiful things blowing across the street onto her cement garden. It is the wind sweeping up lost things for her inspection, things that still need to be touched, owned, approved. She would love to be lost this way, completely lost, never finding her way home.

She had not felt the postcard at first, as the circulation at her feet is poor, but she heard it tapping at her feet, impatiently. She had been looking toward the sky, past the clothesline next door, listening again to the dots and dashes, and was lost in another idea; that a portrait should be painted of her at her sunny writing desk. It would be so easy for an artist to substitute flowers and trees and she could be anywhere. Anywhere is a very special spot, Evangeline realizes.

Bending down to pick this postcard up, she feels an everyday kind of terror that dances down her arms. But it is only a small dread, a gift of zeros, that makes her heart stutter. This postcard is a magic gift. She is certain. As she delicately holds it up to her eyes, Evangeline decided to read the back first, then study the picture on the front. She will find room in the back of one of her books for this card. The address is smudged, but she can definitely make out where this card is from:

TARJETA POSTAL
"Vista Color"
Lito en Mexico

Then at the bottom:

*Yelapa es un lugar y abunda las Iguanas
y Garrobos, aqui un ejemplo en manos de
un nine.* Yelapa is a peaceful place
with plentiful iguanas as this specimen
in the hands of a child.
PUERTO VALLARTA, JALISCO, MEXICO   FOTO: TPM

Evangeline smiles. In the hands of a child. Puerto Vallarta, Mexico, is a place she's seen before. Acapulco with its windy sea and beaches of undertows. Brochures of Guadalajara and its baroque streets. And now this Yelapa and Puerto Vallarta. This is a magic she understands. Evangeline relishes this and turns the card over, then closes her eyes, realizing she hasn't read the message on the back. Things must be done in order, and the picture comes last. Slowly she opens her eyes again, and reads the message.

Dear Keith—
Billy's skin lesions are spreading and we have to fly back
to San Francisco. Also he is having problems breathing. I
think it is the end. Puerto Vallarta is beautiful, surely
heaven on earth. Will be home in one piece, AIDS or not.
All my love. I miss you.

TOM

Evangeline is chilled, even now in the sun. She is never
sure how death works, or about her own. She remembers
how she rode a bus for thirty-five years, the long straight
ride down Wilshire Boulevard to Santa Monica and the sea,
and knew the bus driver, a woman named Lucille, who always remembered Evangeline's special days, like birthdays
and Easter. Then one day Lucille looked at Evangeline, right
in the eyes, and said, "See you later, Evangeline, I've decided next week is the week I die, so best wishes and take
care of yourself." And she did. Evangeline admired her sense
of order, and knew Lucille was traveling.

She wonders if Billy is already dead, about what he saw,
if he cried staring out into the Sea of Cortez. Did her travelers feel his pain, or were they laughing with him over a
margarita by a pool, saying easy things that comfort, like
you look rested, and change is better than a doctor, and put
it out of your mind. Stare at the sea, Billy. Listen to the sky.
Your ugliness is only passing, then you will not care.

Evangeline shakes this out of her mind. She turns the postcard over and studies the picture. She sees a ten-year-old
Mexican boy with almond-shaped eyes and creamy brown
skin holding a giant iguana. The iguana is alive, electric
green, staring at the camera with prehistoric eyes. The little

boy is smirking; perhaps he doesn't like pictures, or perhaps he doesn't like iguanas. His shoulders are well-formed, and she can tell he will grow into a handsome man.

This little boy has beautiful black hair, soft as the blur in the background. His skin has rich chocolate veneer. Evangeline wonders if he has grown up on the beaches of Puerto Vallarta, under that exquisite, buttery sun. If his family raises iguanas to be stuffed; many of them do, a very respected trade. Does he eat horse meat? Does he smoke hand-rolled cigarettes that he keeps hidden from his mother, who would hit him if she knew? Does he have a soccer ball hidden behind a toilet in the tourist section of Puerto Vallarta, that he takes out to kick with his hands open for American dollars? Does he beg? No. She dismisses all her ideas, judging the arrogance in his young face. Evangeline lets the colors speak. She traces his form with her fingernail, and licks her lips, then swallows.

It is the blur of the photograph that beckons. The white sand behind the boy could paralyze the uninitiated. There are cages in this creamy distance, with iguanas slapping against wire and wicker doors. They are a long walk from the boy, across the sun, the heat and radios, and steam of beef and onions. There is a fuzzy outline of a restaurant on this beach. It has a palm frond roof and people sitting lazily at tiny tables secured with matchbooks. Their legs are bare and oiled.

These are my travelers, Evangeline thinks. Someday I will be one of them. She smiles. I can feel them on my thumb, trapped in this postcard, living in a heat so intense you can lick the air for food.

I am there now, in the heat, the sea, the blossoms of vulgar Mexican flowers that go past decency. Everyone I know is there. The widows are drinking a vile blue drink in the shade, next to an electric fan. A breeze rolls over them and their lipstick is peach gloss. Their skin is hard as the iguanas who eye them from their cages, and their arms are coated with Ban de Soleil and its peculiar aroma. The rich widows play cards, gin rummy, eye the new yachts in the still water and whisper rich women things. Their toes sift through sand. They see me, nod their heads, make a gesture that says, Tonight, Evangeline, tonight. Their gigolos wait. I see the liver spots on their hands as they wave, the diamond rings, the bone underneath.

I see Billy on his ground floor terrace at the Hilton. He waves to me even though we haven't really met. He has a row of prescription bottles on a brass tray next to him, and inside his friend Tom is shouting in an ugly voice on the phone. A light breeze that smells of just-cut fruit washes over Billy's face, and he closes his eyes.

Billy is wearing a blue and white silk scarf over his head to cover the baldness from his chemotherapy, and he undoes it, letting it fall around his shoulders. The air must feel very good to him. I can get an exact picture when I don't squint. He knows I am here, watching over him. He tries to breathe in deep, then convulses and spits up phlegm, keeping his eyes closed.

I know this is the same air that two weeks later will wash over Billy's room at the hospital. He will close his eyes to smell the just-cut fruit of Puerto Vallarta, and the light in his sterile hut will brighten in silence. The scarf will fall on the floor and his mother and sisters will scream.

The mother and sisters will feel something moving behind them and turn, but they will only feel the glow of a late afternoon sun. They will swear, later, that they heard surf, parrots in the hills, children with soccer balls speaking in a different tongue. An odor of melons and oranges. A woman singing.

I am pleased but do not know why. I look further and see others on balconies above Billy and they all seem to know me, and I realize sooner or later everyone gets their balcony overlooking the sea. Some have drugs beside them, others a book or a photograph. Some have a joint, a margarita, and a gun. But it is the lure of the photograph that draws them, sexual as a last breath and infinitely kinder.

I turn my back to Billy, knowing he will be safe here, that it will never get too cold here, or rotten, or dark. The hills framing this beach are tingling with a flushed, pulsing green that screeches like a child who's eaten too much candy.

I walk further. I have an exotic drink with shaved coconut. I know my legs can run, but I decide not to. My white hair blows in the wind. My white hair is the only thing I have ever been proud of in my life, and I am staring at the ships arriving, the sun poised like a hand grenade, the beachboys scratching, grinning, and diving in the surf. The waves in front of me are thin as hotel stationery, and if I open my eyes now they will be in front of me, on my writing desk in my cement garden, but I do not open my eyes yet.

I understand this place. Everything is explained. I understand the scarlet macaw on the bartender's shoulder, the old man masturbating behind a bus who can no longer ejaculate, the women going to market, high-pitched, with large hips and bare, callused feet. Even sound is decisive and regular, telling me not to be afraid. Enter. Live inside me.

He looks exactly like the others I have touched, travelers who stand at the top of the stairs, ready to depart, their destination confronting them like a lover, looking back at me and smiling, their hair tossed in a new, redeemed heat. Over and over I see the faces, the twist in the shoulder, the scenery beyond, the trace of death.

I touch the little boy's shoulder and he turns and smiles at me. This boy thrusts his lizard up for me to see. It is heavy and he almost falls down with the weight of it. The iguana has marbles for eyes, yellow with that common reptilian black slit that studies with the proficiency of stone. Its eyes roll up to me. Its face has tiny horns and it emits a silent hiss, saying, I am abandoned too, Evangeline. I am rolling toward you in the wind, like all good things. Pick me up and pity me, feed me and tell me you love me. We stare at one another. The little boy drops this iguana on the white, white sand and it falls with no sound, like dropping a baby on a soft bed.

He shows me how to walk it on a leash and I laugh. The iguana slowly twists through the sand, making trails like a seismograph. I can hear it saying to the little boy, Take me to my cage. Take me back to my cage. The little boy only giggles, and I see sun caressing his boy-man body.

Here my skin doesn't burn. I am cool with my exotic drink, and blur; I am exact as I will possibly be. I am the older lady who never married. I am the old lady who smiles at the straw markets, smiles near the Aztec ruins, by vivid poolside umbrellas and on balconies of black wrought iron and blacker shutters. I am there to talk to and I know about every undiscovered place.

Evangeline realizes her eyes are closed, and her hands, in an unwilling arthritic claw, have dropped the postcard. There is a sudden heavy wind. The rim of her straw hat is bouncing and soon she will have to go inside.

She opens her eyes to see her postcard carried off in the wind, back into the half gutter, then across the street toward the alley that leads to the apartment complex where last night someone was hot, and she stays at her writing table long enough to watch the postcard walk out of her vision, into another blur, a new palette. Evangeline realizes beyond the blur there is nothing, perhaps sky, certainly no ground or humanity, and once she leaves the serrated edges of this card, she ceases to exist. It's gone. It has blown against someone's door.

Evangeline knows someone will find it and throw it away. The iguana boy will laugh and wait for her. Evangeline feels amazingly light. She stares at the sky and nods her head. Puts a wet finger to the breeze. And plans how to fly.

at the four seasons hotel

"I got a funny story."

A perspiring man in a blue serge suit with a felt cowboy hat and a copper bolo tie, leans over to his companion. He is at least seventy-five years old, and his face is pink, unnaturally healthy. His companion is an Italian about the same age as he, with a high, white pompadour, sprayed so thick with hair spray, bits in the back have fallen off.

They are sitting in the cocktail lounge of the Four Seasons Hotel on Doheny Drive. I am reading quietly in a booth next to them. I like coming here, studying the regulars, never fully realizing I am a regular too.

This is an expensive cocktail lounge, in pale silver grays with Louis Philippe chairs covered in cream damask. Outside, through the French windows, it has been raining, and the dusk light is a rinsed, fading blue, deepening into a California gloom. I realize at this moment I could be anywhere; Paris, Madrid, Hong Kong. Anyplace the hookers are high and the air is tight. The drinks are always the same. The conversations are an obvious language. The light dims quickly into an ebony veneer.

I gaze numbly at enormous floral arrangements in Roman urns. They are the only color in the room, with roses and striped tulips and giant magnolias and gardenias. I signal a waitress, as the flowers are soaking up all the oxygen, and ask her if she could open a set of windows. She agrees. There is no breeze and I can only hear the sound of the two old men sitting next to me.

At the bar I notice a lot of Iranian men in Giorgio Armani suits. Two famous television comedians sit down on stools, hunched over and looking for the girls.

And the girls are here. They arrive in Rolls-Royces, convertible Mustangs, brand-new Cadillacs with speakerphones, front seat computers, and burgundy upholstery. They are here to make money. They have stockbrokers' hearts.

A beautiful Asian girl, about five-foot-two in four-inch heels, keeps walking by me, assessing my possibilities, but pretending to be confused and looking for someone. Of course she is, I remind myself. The old cowboy in the blue serge suit with the funny story tries to get her attention, but she will have none of him, at least not yet. She is wearing a gold patent leather raincoat, cut short and tied at the waist. Her hair is cut in a bob and it is perfectly straight and shining.

I wonder if she is Vietnamese or Chinese. She is too small to be Thai. I also wonder if she is wearing an incredibly short dress under her raincoat, or a pair of hot pants. Or just panties. She snaps her fingers and two waiters appear. With hushed, rapid syllables she hands them two business

cards and points them with a fluttering finger to several Irani-
ans at the bar.

I turn my attention to the two men next to me.

"So you wanna hear it?" the cowboy asks as the Asian
girl disappears to the bar. His friend sucks some saliva
through his teeth and swallows. His voice is high-pitched,
noncommittal.

"Sure." There is a pause. Both men take sips of their
scotch.

"See, there's this guy from Brownsville in Brooklyn.
Named Jimbo. Just finished his second horror picture. Low
budget. Cow guts, old house, blondes with big tits in the
shower. You know the scene."

"Sure."

"Only Jimbo don't tell no one he's taking funds. Sure, he
delivers the picture, it's on budget, but no one knows he's
conned six figures out of it. He gets married, has a kid, real
respectable."

The old cowboy takes his hat off and I see he is bald. He
wipes off the top of his head and puts the hat back on,
then continues.

"Fuckin' hot in here. So, anyways, Jimbo gets the call
from Hollywood. He's supposed to meet Mr. P, big-time
guy, knows everyone in town. Plays tennis with Bob Evans,
for Chrissakes. Jimbo's supposed to be at Mr. P's house in
Bel Air at two P.M. on Thursday. For lunch, no less. Jimbo
gets on the plane in a beige silk suit, black socks, big diamond ring. Good lookin' and ready to move."

"Sure."

I am not sure if the Italian, the White Pompadour, is
merely bored, or speechless with interest. He says "Sure" as

if he means it. That by this one word his opinion of the world is safe.

The old cowboy clears his throat.

"He gets a call on the plane from Mr. P's chef, a Swedish chick named Anna, who says, 'Look, Mr. Jimbo, I fix jumbo grilled shrimp from Mexico for you and Mr. P. I serve it on a bed of lettuce, all different colors. Any color lettuce you like, Mr. Jimbo?' "

I have put down the book I've been reading, or pretending to read, and sip my mineral water, waiting for the cowboy to continue. He seems to like dramatic pauses. This has less to do with his ability as a storyteller than the cumulative effects of the scotch. The Asian girl is not doing well at the bar. Her crossed legs and smile are worth five hundred dollars an hour, but the magic isn't working tonight. The old cowboy shakes the ice in his glass, signaling to the waitress, who is not paying attention.

"Well, Jimbo's thinking he's going to be the president of a studio, you know, the idea someone's calling him, on a plane, about the color of his Thursday lunch lettuce. So he says, 'Wow, like tell me what kind of lettuce you got.' "

"Yeah?" White Pompadour seems interested.

"Oh yeah." I notice the cowboy takes out a thick wallet.

He waves a hundred dollar bill to get the waitress's attention. This works. Half the girls at the bar turn around, including the Asian girl.

"So this Swede starts in. 'Well, we got purple lettuce, we got light baby pink lettuce, yellow endive, delicate red baby cabbage, white lettuce, shredded emerald-green lettuce, flesh-colored lettuce. We got lettuce mixed with flowers you eat. We got orange lettuce from Northern California. I serve big shrimp on three-colors lettuce. You let me know which colors you want.' So Jimbo thinks and thinks, and blurts out, on the plane phone, 'Purple, yellow, and white lettuce!' "

"Catholic, huh?" His friend now seems to be able to clarify thought into speech.

"On this plane, somewhere over Denver, Jimbo asks Anna where she finds so many different colors of lettuce. She says, 'Mr. Jimbo, this is California. I grow them on my ranch in Bakersfield just for Mr. P.' So old Jimbo's just nodding his head on the plane, like dig it. Money. Power."

The Asian girl lights a cigarette, studying me, then reassessing the old cowboy and his friend. Her jungle red nails tap the bar. As the waitress gives them their drinks, the Asian girl nods first to me, then to my neighbor. I turn and look at him. His eyes glitter. He has perfect teeth, probably dentures. He raises his glass to her. It is an economical gesture.

"So Jimbo is pressed, shaved, washed, and eating shrimp in Bel Air on three colors of lettuce. Mr. P is only wearing a white terry-cloth robe and sunglasses. Jimbo doesn't know what to say, except, 'What a great house.' "

"Good opener," White Pompadour mutters.

"And then Jimbo gathers up all his courage and asks, 'Do you want me to work for you? Is that why I'm here?' "

"And?"

By now the bar is crowded and there is almost no air. What is left to breathe careens and lilts with women's laughter and the low whispers of men on the make, men with money who treat this as a game, as if each night is another bead on the abacus.

"Mr. P scratches his balls, stands up, and says, 'You gotta be kidding. You stole my money.' Just like that, Jimbo feels a hand on his shoulder. Mr. P says, 'You little nobody, I wouldn't feed you to my dogs. You stole a hundred grand from me. It's all over, Jimbo.' "

"And?" White Pompadour asks, sipping his new drink.

"Well, I was the hand on Jimbo's shoulder."

"You were always the best. Clean as a whistle."

"Thanks. Real quick I take a table knife to his throat, but it's dull, and I say, 'You're going to have to get these knives sharpened, Mr. P,' and he says, 'I'll make a note of it.' Jimbo's struggling, making all kinds of racket, so I just go ahead and strangle him easy as pie."

My skin chills and I pick my book up. The old cowboy begins to laugh.

"That Mr. P, what a card. He says to me, 'I always like for them to be able to choose the color of their last meal.' "

"How much he pay you?" White Pompadour asks.

"Fifteen thousand."

"Not bad."

"Get this." The old cowboy rests his hand on White Pompadour's shoulder. "So the Swede broad takes poor dumb Jimbo up to her ranch near Bakersfield, buries him, and plants purple, white, and yellow lettuce on top of him, with those little cards next to each plant that tells you their names."

"What a riot."

"I tell you, they're crazy here in California. Great story, huh?"

"Funny. Sure." White Pompadour laughs.

The old cowboy eases back into his French chair.

"It was damn nice to be back on the payroll again, I tell you. It's nice to be appreciated."

I always assumed old killers wound up in jail, or dead, or hidden away by alcoholic women. I think, This is where we all wind up. If we're smart we'll grow old and sit in expensive cocktail lounges and tell hideous tales. We'll have a wallet full of hundred dollar bills.

The old cowboy moves around on his French chair and speaks in a matter-of-fact tone.

"But they got great-lookin' whores in California." He nods to the Asian girl, who looks at me first. I am frightened. I try to shake my head no, don't go to those men. She seems perplexed, and cocks her head sweetly. The two men turn and look at me. Their faces are old and weak, but their eyes cold as brass on a coffin.

I shudder, look at my book, but I cannot decipher words. I look up and see the Asian girl sitting with the old cowboy and White Pompadour. She has ordered a plate of appetizers and is nibbling a piece of white lettuce decorating the side of the plate. The two men look at each other and begin to laugh.

tim

Tim looks into his face in the casket and thinks to himself, I never realized my skin was so white, like marble. The leukemia and chemotherapies had made him bald, his head like a small melon, and Tim laughs.

The room where he is laid out is in a cheap funeral parlor. Tim guesses that all the medical bills have left his mother without money, and that she is trying the best she can, as she always has, as she would whisper to him on especially rough nights.

Most of the guests Tim doesn't know. Most of the guests avoid looking in his coffin, as though a bald dead boy is too much to stomach, or perhaps it is simply too much for the more fainthearted.

There are flies buzzing around, and he sees his maternal grandmother, Sally Ann, swat annoyingly at a horsefly that somehow got in the red-flocked velvet room. His father's parents are here too, and Tim, even though he does not know his father, is glad that Clint and Rosa have come. They have always been very sweet to him, making him laugh.

Tim can smell lemon oil and wood, the heavy stench of two-day-old lilies, the perfume of relatives. In the next room there are sandwiches and sodas and liquor. His mother holds a large glass of scotch, something he's never seen her do, at least not while he was alive.

"Only ten years old," is a general murmur that seeps through the room.

"I am not. I'm almost eleven. One more month," Tim says to the air. A candle flickers briefly.

His mother sits next to his casket, staring at his shell, her eyes red and glazed. She doesn't speak to anyone, but sips her scotch very deliberately. Little tiny sips. The kind of sips, Tim thinks, to make the drink last longer.

"Susan, we are so sorry. But it is a blessing and, I'm sure, a relief." A pair of middle-aged women speak quietly to his mother, who does not pay attention.

"Susan, I'm ashamed of my son. Frank should have been here. I'm stunned. I don't know what to say," weeps Rosa, who puts her hand on Susan's shoulder. Susan takes her hand briefly, then lets it fall away.

"That's Frank. Just the way it is," Susan whispers. Rosa bites her lip, tears streaming down her heavyset face, and nods knowingly.

Tim can discern jasmine incense burning in one of these small, upholstered rooms and remembers when he was five, still healthy, and his mother had taken him into an Oriental gift shop. He was fascinated by the incense, cones and sticks, all the burners to put them in, like little temples, or dragons' mouths.

Tim stands next to his mother. It feels good to stand, to feel so light, but he doesn't like the fact he can't feel, or interact with the living. At one point during the burial that follows, when Tim watches himself lowered into the ground, he tries to knock off the hats of a couple of fat ladies sobbing quietly into small, well-worn lace hankies, but to no avail.

Tim thinks, It's funny, you know, the cemetery is very close to the soccer field. For the last three years of his life, Tim watched a group of boys play soccer every afternoon. His mother had wheeled his bed and oxygen tent over to their second-floor window. They became shimmery figures, seen through the tent's plastic, but Tim knew who they were, each of them.

Tim and Susan used to have a pretty house in the Pacific Palisades. Everything was pretty then; Susan was a pretty "divorcée," always accentuating the end syllable. But when Tim got sick, suddenly it was a two-bedroom apartment at the Tropic West in Van Nuys overlooking that field, and the cemetery beyond, all brown and almost green grass.

The almost green grass is where the soccer players played. Tim knows them by heart. There is the little runt who lives in his building. He can kick a ball like nobody's business, but doesn't run fast enough, his legs being too short.

And then the three muscular boys, already well into puberty, who circle and work the ball with the grace of young bison, or deer hopping up a steep hill. When he was sick, Tim dreamed of running the way they did, all muscle and light, but then he would wake up in a sweat and not be able to breathe.

Tim's father never came around, and he isn't at the funeral today either, Tim realizes with a scowl. He used to send money. Tim remembers Susan screaming into the telephone, pacing back and forth, pleading, begging.

"Do you have any idea of what I'm dealing with here?" was something she said that stuck with Tim. He always tried to be extra nice to his mother. She would kiss him a lot, wipe tears from her eyes, smile then scowl if something was wrong with his bed. When she helped him up to go to the toilet, she was always real nice about not looking at his wiener. He loved his mother.

And still does. Tim runs his hands along his mother's black serge suit as she walks away from the gravesite. Blue-gray clouds are gathering and Tim can feel rain approaching, like a gang of bad news, and he's glad his mother drives the short distance to their courtyard apartment complex.

Tim does notice certain things. He no longer feels cold or heat. He can't walk through walls like Casper the Friendly Ghost, but he can imagine himself where he's supposed to be, and he's there. As he watches Susan drive away, toward home, in her Ford Pinto, Tim makes sure he is in the living room when she gets home.

First he stops by the field where the soccer players have gathered. The sky is a threatening, dusky blue, cumulus clouds edged in black piling up into the distance.

"Gonna rain," the runt says, looking up to the sky.

"Yup." One of the older boys cracks his knees, then spits. "Let's try for a couple of goals. Just for the footwork."

"It's gonna get wet," the runt squeaks.

"So what?"

"I dunno. I saw a kid in my building who just died. He was bald and shriveled and really gross. The sheet slipped and it was like he was looking at me." The runt picks up a blade of grass and looks at it quietly.

"So what?"

"Well, I mean, if it rains cold, we could catch pneumonia and die shriveled up, so I'm going home."

"Chicken." All the big boys made chicken noises.

"I'll see ya." As the runt turns and begins to walk back to the Tropic West, Tim walks alongside him. "I was looking at you," Tim whispers into the suddenly damp wind. "I know everything about you."

When Susan closed the door to the apartment, she unbuttons her tidy little black jacket and tosses it on the sofa, then goes over and pours herself another large, stiff scotch. Tim is entranced. He's never seen her drink. It seems so adult. Susan walks into Tim's room and closes the door. Why, Tim thinks, no one else is here except me.

Susan leaves the lights off. The room is not dark, but filled with the blue light of the oncoming rain. Her face is half in shadow, completely emotionless, her eyes glazed. Tim's tent and IV and other various apparatuses look like amusement park rides in this light. Tim never really saw this before. But then, he occupied them.

Susan sits in Tim's room all night, still, sipping her scotch, silent. Tim sits with her, trying to think of something to say, but he knows she won't hear him.

This continues for many weeks. Tim is never quite sure of time, but he knows his mother is beginning to drink a lot, pass out. Soon she is putting on high heels and going out. One night Tim is stretched out in a corner of the living room and his mother comes home with a man, a heavyset redheaded man in a plaid jacket. They are both incredibly drunk, and the male guest immediately passes out on their green velvet sofa.

This does not fare well with Susan. She clicks her teeth

and whistles, but there is no response. She pours herself a scotch.

"I thought we came here, you and me, to talk. I need to talk. So . . . I'll talk. You just relax and listen."

Snores from the redhead.

"I never really drank, you know, not until my baby died, then it seemed to help. I got no money, nowhere to go, I can't have any more children, and I'm getting too old to get myself a new man. So I drink."

Susan looks around the room.

"You don't know certain things, buddy, you fat prick. You don't know what absolute exhaustion is."

It has begun to rain. Susan presses her nose to the window. The room is almost dark, with the exception of our table lamp that is on, making everything look like a Humphrey Bogart film, Tim thinks. Kind of scary.

"And you will never know what true despair really is."

Susan raises her chin.

"Tim." It is an echo, a piano heard from far away, a bell.

"Yes, Mom, I'm here, I'm with you. Don't worry about a thing. I thought I'd go to heaven, but no one's shown up or told me how it works. I'm sure it works."

Susan shakes her head and weaves her way toward her bedroom, carefully locking the door behind her.

Tim feels bad. This fat greasy man doesn't belong here. Not in his mother's house. Not in *his* house.

Soon Tim is in his mother's bedroom. She has passed out on the bed, facedown on the pink quilted bedspread, one high heel just about ready to fall off her foot.

Tim has never really spent much time in this room. After all, it's his *mother's bedroom,* and when he was sick there was no going inside to snoop around, partly because he was just too weak.

There are pictures of Tim as a baby in heart-shaped silver frames, and even pictures of Tim, bedridden and bald, smiling up at the camera. He notices that everywhere there are mementos of him. It is a room that somehow he *expected,* with the smell of Chantilly, his mother's favorite fragrance, in the walls, and in the bathroom the smell of open nail polish bottles.

Strange, Tim thinks, I don't need to cry. I can laugh but it comes out funny, like a motorbike engine without oil.

Tim can hear the sound of his mother's breathing, a rasp that he doesn't like. He knows it's the scotch, the late nights. He doesn't understand why she would choose to live like this, keeping his room intact and drinking a bottle of scotch every night. It frightens him, but it hurts too. Susan must hurt very much, Tim realizes.

Suddenly, Tim understands what must be done. He lies down next to his mother, as close as he can. Her one high heel falls on the floor. Tim hugs her, then gradually, he slips through her to the inside, first the legs and arms, then the bald head and pigeon chest, as he repeats softly:

"I'm here with you."

The next morning Susan groggily comes to. The red-haired man is pounding on her bedroom door.

"Goddammit honey, come on, let me in."

"Look, buddy, you came over to talk, that's all," Susan yells through the door. "We talked last night. Now please leave."

"The hell I will. Open this door."

"No. Either get the hell out or I'm calling the police."

"All right. All right." There is a long silence and the sound of rustling, then the fat man's voice. He is in Tim's room.

"What the hell is all of this? You running some kind of hospital? Jesus, look at this crap."

There is the sound of things breaking, of pills dropping on linoleum and scattering.

"I'm calling the police right now!" Susan shouts through her bedroom door.

"All right, bitch, but I'll be back."

"Don't hold your breath!"

Susan hears the front door slam, and she gets up from her knees in front of the door and opens the drapes. The sun is intense, like a white bolt of heat made purposefully to knock out women with hangovers.

Susan looks into the mirror and sighs. Suddenly her eyes grow large, brimming with tears. She runs her hand through her hair, then stops. She smells the crook of her neck, her hands, arms, breasts. She begins to cry, then laugh.

"Tim," she says, her voice rising to a pitch. "Tim!"

Frances is furious. It is the end of a windy November afternoon in the San Fernando Valley and she has discovered, through her mechanic of almost twenty-three years, that her 1969 Mercedes is not mustard, but butterscotch. She was pregnant with her only daughter when she first bought this car. She was married, trying to be happy, as her neighbors seemed to be. Frances has always maintained this automobile, like every other salient point of her life, with dedication and care. And she hates the idea she is driving a candy-colored car.

Frances turns the car off in her garage and thinks, You go through life with a mustard-colored car and suddenly you find out it is butterscotch. You go through your life thinking you are an average woman and suddenly you find out the colors you live by have changed.

Perhaps they were never the right colors, she reasons. Perhaps had she worn shades of amethyst during her youth, she wouldn't now be alone. Or pink instead of black. Perhaps if she had worn a deep red lipstick instead of glossy peach, she would have married a different kind of man, one that wouldn't leave. And she would have had more than one child. And murder wouldn't have entered her life; an evil bringing with it a solitude so perfumed with desolation she sometimes cannot breathe.

Perhaps things would still be safe. Frances shakes her head as she walks into her kitchen. Nothing is safe anymore. Except for the end of the day, when no one calls.

Her friends used to call. After her tragedy, she talked on the phone and then stopped answering it. Her friend Lucille was losing a son to AIDS, and would call Frances to ask her what to do. She remembers Lucille in 1970, in a shimmering silver dress, like a flapper, it was a Roaring Twenties party, with her five-year-old son, Kevin, pulling at her dress, his face full of sequined reflected light and his mouth smeared with licorice. Now Lucille is a voice, just a voice, saying, "What do I do, Frances, I don't recognize him anymore, he has no hair, he's only twenty-nine years old, Frances." Frances had no answers.

Another friend, Mona, would call Frances after her husband died of liver cancer and ask Frances to come over and get drunk; Frances declined. Mona repeated herself, like a chant, "You understand death, Frances, you've been there."

Frances realizes all the women she knows are now surviving someone. Like her, they wore bellbottoms at the beginning of the seventies, smoked marijuana and had affairs with red-haired Englishmen who smelled like lavender and were always cruel. They raised their children in converted churches and old apartments, then moved to the San Fernando Valley. They divorced, remarried, changed their furniture every five years. They wore more makeup in the eighties, and shoulder pads, and studied French. They were alcoholics. They tried their hand at poetry and failed. They became religious, desperate, brittle. They frosted their hair, had cosmetic surgery, stopped eating, sued doctors, took up ballroom dancing. Anything for the magic again, Frances thinks. They bury their husbands and children and keep thinking, This wasn't part of the colors I chose, I wasn't meant to survive without signs and clear, impartial directions. These women are fifty years old and invisible as an old homosexual. And they are exactly like me, Frances concludes, except I know the magic.

Frances looks around her living room. Her furniture is precisely arranged, clean and aging. Her cockatiel is waiting for her, and when she enters the room she hears the light rustle of transparent yellow feathers falling to the bottom of its cage. There are other sounds, a half note above silence, that she listens for; the soft bang of the forced air heater in the hall closet, the automatic sprinklers murmuring at dusk, the hardwood floors contracting in the sudden November cold.

She has taken down the photographs of her daughter and packed them in the blanket chest she bought in Marrakesh. Her husband promoted rock acts. It was 1968 and they were on their honeymoon, smoking black hashish in a white and blue tiled house with brass oil lamps and no electricity. She would listen to the shrill morning caws of black-robed women that were indecipherable from birds and cymbals in the markets. She tried to peer through the slits of their black hoods, to see the kohl-drenched eyes the same shape and size as hers, but the light was too intense, the white walls too electric.

It was here her daughter April was conceived. It was on the night astronauts walked on the moon, and radios all over the hot city were turned on to a language no one understood, but everyone was pointing to the sky, to the moon, the sleeves of their caftans waving in the sweet African wind. She was on the roof of her tiled house and her husband was on top of her. She looked past the curly blond hair falling off his neck onto hers and stared at the moon as he thrust. She tried to frame it in her arms, knowing someone was there, calling to her, walking in weightless air.

Frances realizes, as the light begins to crawl away in her living room, that she hasn't traveled since. Except for now, for the last year, when she creates magic. Frances sits in her armchair after turning on the old air-conditioning unit in the den that blows neither hot nor cold, and closes her eyes. She pretends she is on a plane, and slowly constructs her hands and legs, then tilts her head back as though her plane were taking off. Her air conditioner makes the exact whir of a plane's interior, and Frances is hovering over Martinique, Prague, Havana, places she will never get to. Her daughter is with her and pointing to cities clouded in opaque dust. Her daughter is well-proportioned and adult, in a floral cotton dress and sandals. She has clean hands which she pressed to the window, then to Frances' face.

Frances knows that when she opens her eyes now, her house will be silent, bathed in the comfort of pastel shadows. For a moment she has traveled with her daughter into impossibly pale blue Caribbean worlds, where cumuli knock themselves together to shake palms and birth orchids. This past year they have visited the house where April was conceived, islands with volcanoes and granite hotels, and Frances always arrives safely here, to the dusk of her life.

This is an incantation, one of many spells of ordinary twilight, where air assumes its own color, a mauve stirred with tobacco, and light agonizes its departure. Frances never turns on the lights. Frances rises and goes to her bathroom mirror. It is now she is able to see her face, porcelain and devoid of age. She cannot see her eyes and she is pleased. Only a whiteness. It is the time of day for silhouettes and thought without gravity, when she can't feel hot or cold, but moves through a cushioned, easily numbed world, its shading sketched by her own discretion.

This is the time for planning every luxury, then tearing its structure apart. She will have a cigarette, a scotch and soda. She will buy a mink coat, have lunch with her friends. In this winter shade Frances knows that in her life, like the history of a small town, everything and nothing will occur.

Frances murmurs a prayer for April under her breath, making it so light its tone cannot be taken away from the other sounds of her house. This way each spell becomes pure. She turns the air conditioner off and sits back in her armchair, remembering that tonight, as she has read in the paper, is a lunar eclipse. This evening she will converse with the moon, its face like hers in twilight; softened, smaller, devoid of pain.

Frances still cannot remember certain things about her behavior following the death of her only daughter. She remembers there was no Christmas last year. She remembers screaming, having shingles and going to the hospital, then being home again, and discovering that only at dusk she could move around freely, make coffee, apply makeup in the dim swirl of average grays and lavenders.

She does remember her first day out. Barely a month ago, after almost a year of having groceries sent in, of memorizing programs on television. She wore dark sunglasses and drove to Woolworth's in the white straw hat, with veil, she was married in. She bought bubble bath in a champagne bottle, and powder. Then she sat at the counter and had a grilled cheese sandwich with a grape soda in a pointed paper cup in an aluminum holder. She spoke pleasantly with the waitress, who told her Woolworth's was closing down. Frances replied, "Yes, I know, but everything is closed now."

On her way out she bought a cockatiel, cage, and food. In the car, driving home, Frances began to laugh. She said out loud to herself, "This is what older women who've lost everything do; they buy a cockatiel at Woolworth's before it closes and they drive home alone. They run red lights, careful to shield their face from the sun, holding a caged bird and wearing the hat they were married in."

She hasn't given the bird a name, nor intends to. She sat for almost two weeks, feeding the bird at twilight, staring at it for no other reason than the fact it was alive. And the bird stared back.

Then just a few weeks ago, during this queer and somehow satisfactory November, when a persimmon haze hung in her living room like shipyard rope, from the fires that ate Malibu and Topanga, her no name bird began to sing. It walked slowly back and center on its plastic perch and let out clear, perfect notes, a music conceived from silence, her silence, and Frances knew her magic had begun to assemble itself. She remembers she smiled.

Now every evening, before the light is gone, the cockatiel sings. Frances has developed a ritual. She sits in her chair and travels on her plane, April at her side. She goes to the mirror and studies her face, how it has taken on an ivory quality, polished but not yet yellowed, like finely kept Chinese carving. She sits again in her chair, listening to her no name bird. Then she looks out the sliding glass doors and sees how the darkness spreads like lagoon water over her rosebushes and baby palms. How it turns her grass to salt, then a true black, the only black she understands.

She considers what is now safe for someone who is still alive and abandoned. What necessary drives must be made; to the market, perhaps the movies, what day of the week is safest to get the car repaired. Who to start calling again, or not. Frances no longer believes in God, but prays to the earth, the moon, the twilight.

God would never permit her life. Frances knows it is this simple.

Then the final spell. Frances closes her eyes again and goes to April during the last minute of her life. Frances keeps her hands in her lap, and she cannot hear the no name cockatiel's song, the monotony of her sprinklers, or the heater in the hall.

She starts by reciting the facts in a whisper. Her daughter April was murdered one year ago by a stranger, a schizophrenic man who hadn't been under medication. April was twenty-four years old. She had spoken on the phone to her mother about her boyfriend, who had problems with cocaine. She had hung up the phone at eight o'clock in the evening.

She said she would meet Frances for lunch in the Valley the following day.

The man was from Bulgaria. It happened in Orange County, in a similar neighborhood to the one Frances had lived in most of her life. It happened in the last undecided moments of November, when leaves wilt and twilight comes like an unwrapped surprise.

April was walking her dog in front of her neighbor's house. A crescent moon was up, climbing over her street of rolled lawns and jacaranda trees.

This man couldn't speak English and was deaf. How he got to Orange County, to April's cul-de-sac of ten Spanish cottages, from Miami, where he had landed, is still a point of deliberation. The investigation said he walked.

He had no clothes on, and was standing in back of a pepper tree. He could run on grass and not make a sound. There were no dead leaves in California in the fall.

There was a fair wind from the Pacific. As April walked her dog, she could hear television programs from the houses around her. They were built on tiny lots. April had told her mother she wanted to move; she was tired of watching her neighbors undress. She said she wanted an apartment on the beach, with a view of the ocean and nothing else.

This is the moment that Frances walks in the dark. She pictures the man. She sees black hair, a cold, shrunken penis, arms with birthmarks positioned like constellations, eyes possessing no color except the red fright of a wild animal caught by a flashlight. He comes from behind the tree. His black hair is covered with leaves.

Frances cannot breathe. She goes back to the facts. She clears her throat and begins to whisper again, casting a spell over a hysteria that comes from the outside, cutting its way in with scissors and spit.

April was found strangled under a hydrangea bush, in the front of her neighbor's house. Her neighbor had planted nails in the soil under the bush to make its blooms turn indigo and bright purple.

April had not been touched except for her neck. But the dog had been cooked and eaten in a vacant lot a quarter mile away.

Frances sees a night wind rippling like chiffon used in early silent films to suggest a sea under a cardboard ship. She sees April lose her balance, her hand touch a pair of buttocks, then slide down to the grass. She sees April's knee twist and convulse. A crescent moon passes slowly through an ocean of stars. A cough, then a hack like an unfinished heave. Then a dog barking, running. She sees April's hair caught in leaves and flowers colored by rusting metal. Then a man's bare feet running through wet grass. Then the sudden glassine of April's eyes catching the glitter of a night sky.

Frances opens her eyes. Twilight is over and it is later than she thought. Her no name cockatiel has stopped singing and is pecking at seed. She realizes she has been crying, and that is part of the spell. She rubs the tears back into her eyelids and upper cheeks, like a balm, so her eyes are a hideously clear white. This, Frances knows, is the exorcism. The plea and penance, the eating of shadows and darkness.

She has held April's hand for one year. She has stroked April's hair and kisses her forehead every twilight, murmuring, "Nowhere is safe, sweetheart, we're targets and we don't seem to know why. I made mistakes, April. I should have moved us to New England or Montana, where they say it is safe, but I thought California was warm and exciting and rich. He didn't know you, April, and he was sick and hungry and naked and wild. I have seen others like him, April. They are everywhere, and I don't understand where they come from. They don't speak our language, April, and I am frightened, frightened to leave my house, frightened to wake up."

Frances opens her sliding glass doors and walks out into her backyard. The moon is out. She cranes her neck up, feeling a warm vacancy in her chest and loins, the same feeling she had after delivering April. She almost smiles. This moon is not unlike her face caught in a dusk-draped mirror, the line of light fading around her chignon, her eyes two marble balls, so very smooth. In her twilights there are no lines on her face. Acts of defiance and magic are stretched like old velvet, creating their own brief dust.

This is the safety of ritual. Frances concludes, with a sudden satisfaction, that there are other women like her tonight, counting their dead and looking up to a lunar eclipse. They stand singular and ill-tempered in their backyards, on their balconies and at their bedroom windows. Each day is an ache, and they only have the twilight and subsequent night, if they are smart enough to know what to do with it.

Some, like Frances, have stored their violet resolutions of twilights and are beginning to come out, for lunar eclipses, brushfires, and subtropical winters. They walk with the same rhythm of their forced air heaters, knocking regular and gentle in the hall like an unexpected guest, or the drumlike pink drip of their car's radiator, Mercedeses and Eldorados and Buicks in butterscotch and sea-mist green.

Some are standing, shielding their eyes in the night, thinking they will harm their vision, but this is not the sun. This could never be the sun. Some are lurching toward this absence of light like a spider missing a leg, wearing caftans and lingerie, dampening and scratchy in November air. They conjure their missing in half-lit rooms with locked doors and open windows. They are at bus stops leaving their groceries on the sidewalk, coming out of movie theaters with gloved hands and a purse full of barbiturates. They are all staring at a darkened moon, wanting to float up, leave their keys and houses behind, if only to retrieve what they woke up and lost.

a rumor of prayer

Helen has frosted blond hair that she can barely run her fingers through, but this afternoon she does, in the cool celadons of a no-name hotel room on the beach. It is always a hotel on the beach, she thinks, where you soon step out of your life into mirrors with bad light and tiny wrapped soaps you won't save.

She knows certain things as she opens the slat blinds and peers out onto high tide. She knows she's three blocks south of a freeway turnoff and Los Angeles is two hours away, north, through haze and retirement towns shrouded in mists that just burned off. The sun is cold. It is always cold on the beach. And to Helen it is fair. Deliberate and almost caustic, but fair.

Helen travels on bodies like postcards. She understands the lure of balconies, exhausted beds, and undertows. She loves boys of sixteen, seventeen, with still fluffy patches of pubic hair and pink necks. She likes to find them on these beaches and seduce them with only her eyes. Helen refuses to use body language even though she is proud of her fine hips and firm, oval breasts. She knows these boys will not see where her face has been pulled back, the collagen, the expert knives and the weeks of sitting in dark rooms in desert resorts. They always remark how blue Helen's eyes are. Sometimes, when they are on top of her and she has her breasts pushed together, when their small full lips are open for her and their crucifixes are flopping on their chests, they even tell her they love her.

She always asks them to withdraw so she can watch them shudder and ejaculate. She loves the feeling of their semen running down her breasts and legs, of the way their young men's bodies spasm and hold the moment. Helen knows she will never see them again, but she will live inside them, to be used over and over again; that with their first, perhaps second wives, they will still see her, and that will keep them hard, strong, wicked.

It is that kind of afternoon, and Helen stands naked at this anonymous, surf shook window, seeing herself age quietly in the reflection of the sea. The young man behind her has a funny name she will remember when she is driving home. He is asleep, almost eighteen, with a small pigeon chest and a large, curved penis. Helen made him come twice. She told him that he was strong and handsome, that he was the most romantic man she'd ever seen. Asleep he is not beautiful at all, but destined to occasional chances, a rumor of prayer and a woman who might love him for reasons Helen cannot imagine.

Helen reaches in her purse and walks over to the oak-framed mirror. She applies her lipstick, a silvery pink she has used since she sat on the beach when she was sixteen, covered in coconut oil and Tigress perfume. It was how she met her only husband, and it is the beach she always returns to, the whispers and ice plants and sand in the carpet. And the young men, selfish and innocent with salt in their hair and no plans.

She talks to herself in the mirror, so lightly she can barely hear herself, then to the boy, who has never made love in a hotel room and is dreaming, his eyelids twitching and his fingers tapping sheets like the blind reading aimlessly. Helen is telling him silently from across their lives that he will never amount to much; that he might have children, a woman who will stay by him, forgive him.

As she hooks her brassiere she whispers that he will probably never understand what it is to be kind to a woman, that as he ages he'll fuck to cause pain, that he'll miss the poetry. But that now, with her, he had one good moment. Save it forever. Remember it when someone touches your thighs the way I did. Remember me when you're fifty and you're paying a young girl in a room like this and your wife is driving through clouded roads away, into deliberate days, away from you into a light she can remember.

She looks at him and says without forming syllables the same words she has used before: You will never really love. As she slides on her wraparound silk dress and rotates her feet into her beige high heels, Helen sings lightly to the sleeping boy. Make your hands waves that shudder in psalm, she sings, assemble your words like sweet peaches to peel, pray for me and I'll pray for you.

Helen is back together again. Finding her car keys, she sits on the bed and runs her finger along the boy's sunburnt legs and up through his patchy pubis. She knows he will wake to an empty room. It will be night, and people will wonder what has happened to him. He will think of his mother, his friends, then of her. He will masturbate and look out the window at the rough-lit beach. Then he will hurry away, embarrassed at leaving the keys at the front desk. Someone will say, We hope you and your mother enjoyed your stay, and he will flush, excess semen straining his pants, and nowhere in his nights will he find arms that smelled like Helen's, or what she taught him. He will believe he has become a man even though it is twenty years away. He will believe women are meant to be taken, that they like men's genitals. He will live on jokes that make him feel strong, and when his son is born he will cry but not know why. And every time he meets or hears a woman named Helen, he will pause, if only for a moment, and focus his eyes to a spot that no one around him can see.

"It's appalling, isn't it?" Helen finally whispers into his pierced ear, almost covered by reddish-brown hair. The sun is dimming, and the heavy blanch of fog that caresses one-hotel, seaside towns is spreading like a precise good night. Helen closes the door. Once in her car she will remind herself of exits and turnoffs, avoiding the four o'clock jam on the San Diego State Freeway. The fog will thicken and Helen will search for signs, like other women traveling, arriving evacuated and breathless to names they forget, men they judge by the hour. Helen will try to remember the boy's name. She will say a blessing for him.

Helen lights a cigarette and stares into the rearview mirror, thinking that she is waiting for the one last man, the venereal season, the final I love you.

Tonight I will mention to my husband that I would like

to meet him in Europe, that perhaps we could spend several days together, and he will make an excuse and I will smile. I will touch the end of my breast, circling the nipple with my finger as I put down the receiver, Helen thinks. And all the young men from my beaches will be in my living room with me, naked and gentle and frightened. They will talk to me in the voices of young dogs; I will remember every name and their innocence, the narcotic, the reality that comes after it.

Someone will remember me, Helen reasons. What I look like. How I dance. How I kiss. And in a powdered silence Helen disappears into the wet, soft gray road, her breath a shadow that staggers lips held apart, waiting for a last moment of sun, like a flower of fire, to open and smoke the sky.

tina in the back seat

Tina puts on her stretch lace panty hose but she can't get the lines running up the back of her leg right. At least even. It's cramped quarters, Tina thinks, and these panty hose aren't even mine. Tina runs her hand through her hair and tries to remember which house she took the panty hose from. She can't.

Across the limousine, in a comfy corner seat with an overhead reading light, the man is putting on his shoes. Tina realizes the chauffeur must have seen them. Heard them.

His pants are still at his knees.

"You should pull your pants up before you try to put your shoes on," Tina says quietly, lighting a cigarette.

The man waves his penis at her. "Until we meet again." The man then hikes up his trousers and begins to arrange himself, smoothing out his cuffs and hair.

"A singing penis. That's nice," Tina says, looking out the window.

"Comb your hair, honey," the man whispers quietly.

"Oh year, sure," Tina says vaguely. She takes another drag on her cigarette, then spits into her palms and runs both hands through her coal black hair.

"Better?" Tina says. She is looking at the chauffeur, who is looking at her through mirrored frames. And he's driving at night. Tina pauses. That's cool. Way cool.

She does know where she is. Somewhere on Wilshire in Beverly Hills, headed for the Peninsula Hotel. With a middle-aged salesman named Herbert Halstead, alias Herb the Verb to his friends. Whom she met tonight, standing in her stretch lace panty hose and her little black silk dress. On a street somewhere near the Pacific. In the fog.

Tina likes to get out in the fog. She had just taken the black silk dress from Marcia's apartment, where she stayed overnight, and also took a Chinese beaded evening bag filled with amphetamines, money, and cigarettes. Tina likes to get in the first car that stops for her. Tina likes to be in motion for days and weeks. She knows at some point during this little adventure, her fifth over a two-year period, that she will wind up on a plane going to Central America, maybe Panama City, with a millionaire, maybe that, and she'll just keep on going. She will replace her speed and evening bags from Peking and Marlboro cigarettes for more beaded things, more drugs, anything she lays her hands on that she likes. And she won't stop.

She pulls out vermilion-red lipstick and a small jade hand mirror. She crosses her legs.

"I hope I didn't stain your dress when I . . ." The man stops speaking. He is watching Tina methodically put on her lipstick. One of the spaghetti straps on her little black dress is broken and her breast is almost popping out.

"Did you use a towel afterward?" Herb the Verb says to Tina. She nods sullenly.

"I think so. I can't remember," Tina says noncommittally.

Outside, the Christmas lights of Beverly Hills are sparkling through the tinted glass of the limousine's windows and sunroof. The man seems slightly belligerent.

"Jesus, you can't remember?"

Tina disregards his remark. Her eyes become wide.

"Where'd you get those shoes?" Tina asks. Herb looks down at his shoes.

"Cleveland."

"Oh, Jesus, of course," Tina says acidly.

They are pulling into the Peninsula Hotel's motor court.

"You're a beautiful, beautiful girl. I wish my wife wasn't here with me, or you could stay with me."

"You mean I can't stay in your room?"

"Well, no."

Tina seems bewildered. The man looks at her, getting out his wallet as the limo comes to a halt.

"Here's five hundred dollars, honey."

"I'm not a whore."

"Well, what do you—"

"I said, I'm not a whore."

"Okay. Okay." The man looks at Tina with saddened eyes. "You don't have anyplace to stay tonight, do you?"

"No."

Tina sleeps in the street, in cars, on planes, in guest bedrooms and hotel bedrooms, in shacks, and, once or twice, mansions. It does not matter, Tina thinks. It's the going that counts.

"Take the money and get yourself a nice room, pretty girl."

Tina can see the chauffeur looking at her through the rear-view mirror. Is he an Indian? Tina wonders. She decides he's an Apache.

"Tell you what, Herb, you give the driver the money and let me have the limo all night."

The chauffeur seems alarmed.

"All night?" he says from the front seat. His voice is deep.

"All night," Tina says with resignation. Herb shakes his head and gives the driver the money.

"We're *going* somewhere now," Tina says brightly.

Herb scowls. "I don't get it."

"I like to keep moving," Tina says matter-of-factly. Herb begins to open the door, and Tina is prepared for the rush of cool air, the sudden obvious noises of life.

"You don't care, do you?" Herb says, awestruck. "You don't care what happens to you." Herb eyeballs Tina. "If you were a guy you'd be a bum. You're a drifter."

As Herb gets out of the limousine, Tina slams the door shut, then rolls down the electronic window.

"Mister, I don't drift. I fly." Tina rolls the window up. The chauffeur laughs, and the limousine purrs into a roll.

The chauffeur and Tina begin driving.

"Where are we going, lady?"

"My name's Tina."

"Tina. Where are you going?"

"East. Start driving east. To the desert. The Springs. We'll see the lights of downtown on our way out. That'll be nice."

"I got some tapes here in the front. You want to listen to music?"

"Sure."

"I got the Gypsy Kings. I got Marvin Gaye. I got Annie Lennox."

"Marvin Gaye."

Tina listens to Marvin Gaye singing "I Want You." The limousine is riding smoothly on the Santa Monica Freeway due east.

"What's your name?" Tina lights another cigarette, takes an amphetamine and washes it down with the remains of Herb the Verb's bourbon and ginger ale. She studies the driver. He must be twenty-five, tops. Lots of white teeth, deep beard.

"Running Leg."

"What?"

"My name's Running Leg."

"Me Tarzan, you Jane," Tina says smugly, then stares at the black carpet near her seat. There are semen stains that she rubs away with her left foot, then looks into the driver's rearview mirror.

"What tribe?"

"Navajo. I'm from Arizona."

"I passed through Phoenix once."

"I'm sure you did."

"I like to go to different cities. For no reason at all, you know?"

"No reason at all." Running Leg repeats her phrase over and over, licking his lips as though they were coated with marmalade. He grins. "I'm not real big on city life, Tina. I like the mountains. The sky."

"Oh God, you're not going to give me any of that nature is God, the white man took our rivers and valleys crap, are you?" Tina taps her nails on the polished wood sides of the cabin. She wants to go faster. She wants to go as fast as the limousine will go, faster than blood through a crippled vein, than a heartbeat. Faster than a hummingbird's wings when it flies.

"No, I guess no crap." Running Leg loosens his tie and takes off his chauffeur's cap. Long thick black hair falls out. He shakes his head, and puts his foot on the gas.

"Great hair, Tarzan," Tina mumbles.

"Here's downtown. All lit up. Then on to the desert."

Tina's blood is beginning to rush.

"Cool. How fast are we going?"

"Fifty-five."

"Make it seventy, and I'll relax."

"You got it, Tina." Running Leg puts both hands on the steering wheel. Tina loves how the limousine drags its long body with no sound at all. "How old are you, Tina?"

"Twenty. That Marvin Gaye tape is finished. Put on the Gypsy Kings for a while," Tina orders. She begins to reapply her mascara, taking a Kleenex and wiping away the smeared areas around her eyes.

"So how old are you, Running Leg?"

"I'm twenty-five. I own this car. I own this business."

"That's nice."

"It works." Running Leg coughs, then looks at Tina again through the rearview mirror. "You're very pretty, Tina."

"Thanks." Tina stops for a moment and looks at Running Leg. "So, how much did you see?" she asks quietly. Running Leg laughs.

"Everything. He had a fat hairy ass and no penis, Tina. My ass is much firmer, smooth like a baby, Tina. And I have much more penis than that."

"Good for you," Tina says. "Also, Running Leg, is there an airport in Palm Springs?"

"I think so." Running Leg frowns.

"So tell me, Tarzan, what did you think? Did you enjoy yourself while you watched?"

"No, I don't do that."

The Gypsy Kings begin playing, and Tina loves the wailing voices, the slithering Spanish guitars. It seems to her she is in a cabin on a ship, moving swiftly and silently through a dense L.A. fog, creating its own tunnel in and out of the city. Waves lit by a hazy moon are beneath her, cut precisely by her ship's prow. She takes another amphetamine.

"You should be careful with those, Tina. Do you know what you're taking?"

"No."

There is a silence between the chauffeur and the passenger. As the limousine heads toward the desert, the fog dissipates and Tina can see through the roof that there is a full moon. Running Leg seems to know what she's thinking.

"Like a blue sun, lighting the night," says Running Leg.

"White grass, black shadows," says Tina slowly. "When the grass outside is white by the moon, you got a full moon."

"Who told you that?"

"Nobody." Tina's mother told her that.

"Where are you from, Tina?"

"No place in particular." Tina's mother told her about the white grass of a full moon when she was ten years old. Tina's mother left her when she was eleven, at a train station in Lincoln, Nebraska, in the snow. Her mother patted Tina's hair and spoke quite casually.

"Baby, it's time for you to travel. People will always take you wherever you want to go, remember that. All you got to do is ask. Take whatever you need, Tina. You won't see them again." Tina remembers steam from the train. Tina remembers crying. Then a man who said he had kids at home asked her if she was lost, and she looked up at the sign above him and it said, in large blue letters, "Miami, Florida," and Tina told the man she was supposed to meet her family in Miami, Florida, but she didn't have enough money. The man gave her the fare, and smiled like someone impressed by his own good deeds. Tina took the train to Miami. This was easy. Her mother was doing her a favor.

Tina learned how to read and write when she was with a foster family in Boise, Idaho. She had just turned fourteen, walked out the front door to the highway, past fields of whispering corn bleached a light green by the sun, and a car stopped in about five minutes. She got in.

It was a fat red-haired man named Ed, who asked Tina if she would take her clothes off in the front seat. Tina thought for a moment, said, "Sure," and stripped. Ed began to breathe heavily, and suddenly the Pontiac Grand Prix with racing stripes and a creme vinyl top swerved on the empty highway and came to a stop in the middle of the road. Ed had had a heart attack and was dead, it seemed, so Tina rolled his body out onto the pavement and took his big white shirt, which made a cute dress when she used his belt and put on her pair of pink tights. She took Ed's money, almost five hundred dollars, and his wedding ring and a pinkie ring, which she put on her one silver chain around her neck. She got back into the Grand Prix, watched the cornstalks shiver and shake for a few minutes, looking out for a horizon, then gunned the car and drove west until the gas ran out.

"Where's no place in particular?" It was Running Leg's smooth voice, cutting through her dreams.

"Like I said," Tina's face is flushed.

She wants Running Leg, she wants him on top of her, inside of her. She wants to smell his sweet young man's breath, but she doesn't want the car to stop.

It is dark now in the Inland Empire, and the limousine drives past Banning and Beaumont and blue lit trailer parks with piles of sagebrush that haven't been cleared.

"Tina, look at the hills. No trees. We are coming to the low desert. Soon we make the descent," Running Leg says with a half-interested smile.

"Suddenly you're a tour guide?" Tina hisses. Her eyes are glazed. She looks beautiful in the half-light of the limousine. She reaches into the Chinese beaded bag and pulls out a prescription bottle, small and white. Inside, she takes out a tiny pill.

"What are those?" asks Running leg.

Tina looks at the pill closely.

"White Cross. I think."

Running Leg grins.

"I took White Cross when I was a kid. I remember losing my virginity to Sylvia Blackfeather behind the school at the reservation. I was taking White Cross and drinking beer."

"Good for you," Tina says with a wave of her hand. She lights another cigarette and stares out the window. She likes the way whole valleys and mesas and mountains, lit with the occasional flame of some far-flung ranch house, are passing behind her. Everything is a past moment. There is only what's ahead on the road.

Tina turns back to Running Leg.

"Will you lose your virginity to me, tonight, Running Leg? All over again? Like we were thirteen or fourteen and we just figured it out?"

Tina's voice is tired but her eyes are alert. Running Leg grins.

"Sure, I guess so."

Tina seems satisfied. As the limousine passes by the giant plaster dinosaur and Hadley's Orchard pecan and nut store, a sudden intense wind rattles the car.

"What the hell is that?" Tina asks, her hands shaking.

"Wind. We're in the desert, Tina. Look up through the roof. You can see every star that ever was when you're in the desert."

"Make the car go faster."

"Okay."

Tina peers out through the window.

"What are those?" she asks.

Stretched out before them are thousands of small white metal windmills, dotting the desert floor like broken shale, and lit by ground lights.

"Those give Palm Springs its power, Tina. Electric lights. Air-conditioning. They never stop turning, see, because the wind never stops. Sometimes it's light, sometimes its real heavy, but the wind never stops."

Tina can see the lights of Palm Springs glistening in the far distance.

"Let's stop here. I don't want to go to Palm Springs. Drive

the car off the road and park under the windmills. Then you come in the back, with me."

Running Leg nods his head.

"And by the way, don't think I'll remember you. You're just part of the road," Tina says quietly.

"Just part of the road," Running Leg repeats in a whisper, then slows the car down as it veers off the highway and into the desert.

"I bet you remember everyone you meet, don't you, Tina? Like someday you'll write a book."

Tina stares at Running Leg with a startled, almost innocent expression.

"Why? What for? No, Tarzan, I don't remember anything. And I won't remember you."

The windmills wake Running Leg up. It is a windy desert morning, just a little after dawn, and he listens to their whoosh and clatter. Running Leg notices the sand piling up in the window grooves of his limousine. He also notices Tina is gone. He gets up, naked, and opens the cabin door, wiping the sand off with one of the paper cocktail napkins from the bar. He stands outside his limousine and takes a long pee, then rubs his nude body to get the blood going, and looks up toward the sun and yawns.

He looks around the highway. The windmills are furiously spinning, thousands of them all crisp and white. Down the road he can see, quite clearly, Tina. Her spaghetti strap is still broken and her hair is tossed into a thick black web by the breeze. She is wearing sunglasses and holding her little Chinese evening bag. She is drinking one of the airline bottles of scotch that Running Leg keeps in the limousine's bar.

Tina, in four-inch black patent leather heels, is pacing the side of the road like a panther, her dress clinging and rippling on her body.

From the opposite direction Running Leg sees an old burgundy Mercedes sedan slow down as it nears Tina. She walks over to the driver's side window. A few words are spoken, and she gets in. Running Leg hops back into his car as the Mercedes speeds by, as he does not want to be seen naked. Peering through the tinted glass of the limousine, which turns everything a dark green, Running Leg sees a heavyset German woman with stiff, white-blond hair driving, chatting and smiling. Tina still has her sunglasses on, and she is sitting in the back seat, smoking a cigarette.

Several of these stories have been previously published:

"Baby Liz" in *Story,* Winter 1997.

"Mother of Pearl" in *The Yellow Silk,* 1997, and *Best American Erotica,* 1998.

"Iguana Boy" in *The Olympia Review,* Fall 1997.

"The Spells of an Ordinary Twilight" in *Story,* Autumn 1998.

"A Rumor of Prayer" in *The Rain City Review,* Winter/ Spring, 1994–95.

"Tina in the Back Seat" in *Harper's,* June 1997.